THE ANG

Aton heard a faint shuffling noise. He looked around quickly for anything that would serve as a weapon. He saw a rock the size of his fist and reached for it.

Suddenly there was a thrumming sound and a huge, shadowy form came charging into the chamber. Huge talons grabbed Aton's arms. Foul breath enveloped him. Aton hurled the rock at where he guessed the thing's eyes might be, then struck out with his fist. There was a roar of anger. Teeth like sabers gleamed in the dim green light. Something hard struck the side of Aton's head, and his vision dissolved into night. Images flowered before him: he saw the cave, saw the cave embedded in the planet, saw the planet turning through space. But space was white, a glaring light that burned his eyes, and the stars were black dots pinwheeling around him. . . .

Piers Anthony's Worlds of *Chthon*

Plasm

by
Charles Platt

A SIGNET BOOK

NEW AMERICAN LIBRARY

Copyright © 1987 by Piers Anthony Jacob

SIGNET, SIGNET CLASSIC, MENTOR, ONYX, PLUME, MERIDIAN
and NAL BOOKS are published by NAL PENGUIN INC.,
1633 Broadway, New York, New York 10019

First Printing, October, 1987

1 2 3 4 5 6 7 8 9

PRINTED IN THE UNITED STATES OF AMERICA

For P.A.J.
with thanks

Author's Note

This is a sequel to the novels *Chthon* and *Phthor* by Piers Anthony, and refers to many of the characters and environments introduced in those books. At the same time, however, *Plasm* tells a self-contained story that can be read and enjoyed on its own.

The reader is asked to remember that this is a science-fiction adventure containing characters who should not be seen as role models in the real world.

Contents

In Chthon

On Minion and Beyond

chapter 1 _____

He felt burning muscle-pain, frigid air cloaking his flesh. Aton opened his eyes to a dim green glow, and found a shadowed face above him.

The man's breath was faintly warm on Aton's cheek. "It will take time," he said. The words echoed. Aton felt cold stone under his shoulders and saw a roof of rock overhead.

The man's face receded, and the sharp-nosed, bearded profile was outlined for a moment in luminescent green. *Bedeker*, Aton realized. He had known Bedeker, before. . . .

The thought trailed off. Where there should have been memories, Aton found emptiness. Amnesia: total and frightening.

He tried to roll over. Each little movement hurt him; he felt as if he had been dragged back from death.

"I'll see you again," said Bedeker, moving away.

"Wait!" The word was a rasping sound in Aton's throat. "Where—"

"You have returned to Chthon." Bedeker smiled, and his teeth gleamed in the dimness. He turned, then, and disappeared down a passageway that led out of the cavern. Slow, measured footsteps faded into silence, broken only by faint trickling, dripping sounds in the far distance.

Aton struggled to sit up. *Returned to Chthon.* The statement prompted a sudden cascade of memories. Chthon: a planet honeycombed with caves and lava tubes, forming a vast underground prison. This environment was not alien to him after all; he knew it well. The patches of dim green phosphorescence on the walls of rock were lichen, the sole source of light in this underworld. The rough tunic he wore was a convict's uniform. No one needed to wear anything more than that, down here in the garnet mines where the heat—

Aton paused. He recalled stifling heat, yet the air in here was bitingly cold. He remembered the smell of dust and the noisy camaraderie of miners chipping rock, yet now he was alone. Why did everything seem so terribly wrong?

There was a faint shuffling sound. Aton held his breath and listened, wondering if Bedeker was returning. But the figure he saw creeping into the chamber was a woman: even in the semidarkness, he could make out the shape of her breasts under her convict clothes.

She saw Aton and froze, staring at him. Then she lunged forward.

Feeling weak and defenseless, Aton brought up his arms to protect himself—then realized she was not attacking him. An ax with a crude stone blade was lying beside him on the rocky floor. Such a weapon would be rare and valuable in these empty caves. The woman seized it, retreated, and appraised it, nodding to herself. Then she paused and waited, watching him.

Slowly, Aton struggled up onto his feet, feeling some of his strength returning. He held out his hand. "Give it back," he said.

She raised the ax and eyed him without fear. Her body was statuesque and muscular, and she was almost his own height. In his weakened condition, he was unsure whether he could deal with her. Tentatively, he moved forward.

She read his intention in his eyes, and swung at him. He dodged, but his reflexes were slow and his movements were clumsy. The flat of the ax blade smacked against Aton's shoulder, jolting him backward.

The blow triggered unexpected rage. He yelled and threw himself at her, and the suddenness of the assault took her by surprise. She lashed out once more but he ducked under her arm and fell against her, pinning her against the wall of the cave. He felt supple flesh squirming under rough cloth, her breasts pressing against his chest.

Aton seized her wrist before she could strike again. She made a fist with her free hand and hit the side of his face. He winced, but held on. She bared her teeth to bite his arm. He seized her throat and used finger and thumb to press deep where he judged the carotid arteries should be. She struggled, but he began to feel her weaken.

His victory was brief. He heard voices behind him, then shouts and running feet, and then hands were grabbing him, turning him, throwing him against the opposite wall. He cried out with the impact and found his arms pinned behind him. Someone tied a strip of cloth around his wrists and pulled the knots tight.

His captors turned Aton to face them. He felt blood trickling warm and wet from a fresh wound in his forehead. His pulse was thudding hard, now, and the residual pain in his muscles was masked by the hot rush of adrenaline. He blinked in the dimness and saw fifteen or twenty figures crowding into the small space: men and women, barefoot, wearing convict clothes like his own.

Aton's arms were gripped by men each side of him. The woman he had struggled with pushed to the front of the crowd, moving with an air of authority, holding the ax he had tried to recapture. Her black hair was parted in the center and pulled back, revealing a cruelly beautiful face with high cheekbones. She had finely chiseled features, pale skin, a proud, wide mouth. "Now," she said, studying him closely, "you'll start by telling us who you are."

It would be futile for him to invent a story. He had so few memories, it would be impossible to lie coherently. "My name is Aton," he said finally, and said nothing more.

The woman lifted the ax and touched the corner of its blade against Aton's chest. She dragged it downward, ripping a long, shallow wound in his skin. He tried to pull away, but the rock was sharp and hard behind his shoulders, his wrists were still firmly tied, and the men either side of him kept their hold on his upper arms.

"You can tell me something more useful than that,"

she said dispassionately, watching him flinch from the pain she was inflicting.

He shook his head.

She glanced at his powerful body, then back at his face, and gave him a faint, ironic smile. Without warning, she jerked her knee up into his groin. Sucking pain rolled up through his belly.

"Who are you with?" she demanded.

"No one." The words came out with difficulty. No point in mentioning his glimpse of Bedeker bending over him; it would only create more questions that he couldn't answer.

She shook her head. "It's not possible to survive down here alone."

The statement sparked another brief, flickering memory, this time of a group of convicts on a long march, a hopeless quest in a twilight world of poisonous creatures, starvation, and death.

"What do you think, Jacko?" the woman said, turning to a heavyset convict standing beside her.

He had a square, scarred jaw and a receding forehead. His hair and beard had been roughly trimmed to within an inch of his skin, which looked sallow and oily. "Take him back to the big cave," he said, watching Aton carefully.

She nodded. "Tie his feet. He's stronger than he looks."

"As you say, Oris." Jacko dropped down onto his knees and produced a strip of cloth like the one that had been used to bind Aton's wrists.

Aton could kick the man in the face, and maybe jerk free from the two others holding his arms. Butting with his head, he might be able to charge through the crowd and out of the cavern, into the tunnels beyond. Some of the volcanic rock should be sharp enough to cut the bonds on his wrists, and he would be free.

But the woman named Oris had said that no one in Chthon survived alone, and somehow her words rang true. Aton waited passively as Jacko tied his ankles.

"Groth, Snyder, you carry him." Oris turned without bothering to check that her orders were obeyed. The crowd of convicts made way for her as she strode to the passageway, and then they followed her as she led them out of the chamber in which Aton had been reborn.

chapter ii _____

They carried Aton into a long, wide cavern. It was brighter here: twenty feet above, the roof was thickly coated with glowing lichen.

Oris led the convicts down a rocky slope toward a zigzag gully. A sluggish river flowed in it, disappearing into a deep crack in the cave wall. Great stalagmites, eight and ten feet tall, stood like the misshapen pillars of a ruined monument. Water dripped from the ceiling into pools and puddles scattered across the floor, and the air was misty-damp.

Oris stopped beside the river. "Put him there." She pointed to a slab of rock that was overgrown with dark fungus. Obediently, the men set him down. The fungus was soft, and its cloying moisture seeped through Aton's clothes to his skin.

From where he lay he counted seventeen people in the group. Their faces were lined with grime, their cheeks were hollow, and their shoulders were stooped from years of subsistence underground. Almost all of them were men, muscular but slack-faced and dull-eyed. By contrast, the two or three females were smaller but seemed more alert and assertive.

Oris raised both arms. "Pray," she said.

The convicts bowed their heads. No one smiled.

"Great god of Chthon, guide us." Her voice echoed around the cavern. "Have mercy on us and let us serve you. Speak to us, and we will obey."

There was a long silence. Water dripped; the river made trickling noises beside Aton where he lay on the rock.

"The man we have found," Oris continued. "Was he placed here as a sign?"

More silence.

Oris shook her head. "We'll have to find out for ourselves. Jacko, get on the other side of him."

The big man stepped over Aton and squatted by his shoulder.

"Let's turn him facedown."

Jacko grabbed Aton and flipped him onto his stomach. Fungus pressed against Aton's cheek like a damp sponge.

"Together, now." Oris took hold of one arm and Jacko took the other. With his wrists and ankles tightly bound, there was no way for Aton to resist. They dragged him toward the gully till his head and shoulders hung over the edge. The blood-smeared face that he saw in the surface of the river was framed in long hair turned prematurely gray, the jaw rimmed with white beard. His appearance seemed alien, as if it stared back at him from a distance of centuries.

"Down," said Oris.

She and Jacko pushed hard together on Aton's

shoulders. His face plunged into the river. Water closed over his head.

Instinctively, he struggled; but they gripped him firmly. He kicked his legs until someone sat heavily on them. Luminescent patterns flickered behind his eyelids. He began to feel dizzy, and his chest ached with the desperate need to breathe. He kept his lips clamped tightly shut, but the water was creeping up through his nose, tickling the back of his throat.

After two minutes, Aton's body started to thrash in spasms of its own accord. Panic finally overwhelmed him and he opened his mouth to scream. Water flooded in—

He found himself lying on his side on the fungus-coated slab of rock, coughing and gasping. He retched, shuddered, and took urgent breaths. Slowly, his head began to clear.

"Again," said Oris. She and Jacko grabbed his arms as they had before.

"No!" Aton shouted.

They hauled him forward. Once more, they pushed his head under the surface. This time he writhed and kicked in a delirium, no longer trying to suppress his fear or conserve his strength. He almost freed himself, and had the momentary satisfaction of feeling his feet break loose and his heels smash into something soft and yielding. But then he was losing consciousness, spinning into blackness, as if falling into the chasm of his own missing memories.

This time it took longer to come around. Gradually the roaring in his ears died away and he found himself back on the rocky slab, lying huddled in a fetal position, trembling and coughing up water and bile. Oris was a few feet away, watching expressionlessly.

"Once more," she said.

Aton felt a sudden certainty that they would kill him. He screamed as they hauled him forward—but this time they paused, holding his face inches from the surface.

"If you talk, you will live," said Oris.

"Yes." Aton gasped.

They held him there, waiting.

"I can help you," he stammered. "I know—secrets of Chthon."

Time seemed to stop. Finally, at a signal from Oris, they dragged him back onto the rocks. Aton closed his eyes and rested there, trembling, sick with humiliation. Even now, he had only bought himself a temporary reprieve.

He felt someone loosening the cloth strips binding his wrists. For a moment, his arms were free; then he found himself being dragged backward, till his shoulders bumped up against one of the stalagmites. He leaned against it and didn't try to resist as his wrists were retied behind the calcified column.

His wet hair hung over his face. He shook it aside, spraying water droplets. He shivered as rivulets ran down his neck, across his chest.

Oris stood in front of him. "When he's in a condition to talk, Jacko, you can help me." She turned to the other convicts. "All right, there's work to be done. We're short of food, and we need to scout the area." She quickly divided them into pairs and assigned some to patrol nearby caves in search of game, others to fish in the river downstream. Slowly the convicts dispersed, murmuring among themselves and looking speculatively at Aton as they left.

"Jacko, stay here and watch him. I'll be back in a minute." She strode away.

Aton rested against the stalagmite. He took slow, even breaths, determined to regain control and suppress his fear of what they might do next.

After a minute he looked at Jacko. The man had settled his bulk opposite. He had taken out a mean little knife and was toying with it, his eyes darting toward Aton and back again. The knife was fashioned from rock, but had been painstakingly ground and polished until it was almost as thin and smooth as metal.

"If she's the leader of your group, you must be second-in-command," Aton said.

Jacko said nothing. He used the point of the knife to clean one of his chipped fingernails.

"Oris didn't tell you not to talk to me," Aton went on.

"That's true," Jacko agreed after a moment. "She didn't."

"Where did she go?"

Jacko made no reply.

"Maybe she went to say more prayers to Chthon."

Jacko seemed not to like the tone of Aton's voice. He gave him a sidelong, guarded look.

"I wonder," said Aton. "Does Chthon ever answer?"

Jacko glared at him. "There've been signs. Fire. Water. Creatures."

The last word roused new memories. Aton saw in his imagination a beast like a salamander, whose bite was always fatal . . . a huge mole that fed on lichen . . . a thing that was a cross between a jellyfish and a whale, floundering in an underground pool. He had killed them, once, in order to survive.

"She's saved all our lives," Jacko went on. "A dozen times or more, since we started out—"

"On the hard trek," Aton said in sudden understanding. "You're trying to escape from forced labor in the garnet mines. You're looking for a way to the surface."

"Jacko!" Oris appeared from amid the stalagmites, and the big man scrambled clumsily onto his feet. "Go join the people by the river."

He frowned. "Leave you here?"

"Yes. I'll deal with this."

Grudgingly, he sheathed his knife and lumbered away.

She waited till he had gone, then sat down opposite Aton. She was carrying a bowl crudely carved from rock, and a fist-sized lump of dried meat. The bowl was full of water. The smell of the meat made Aton salivate. His stomach felt bruised and hollow with hunger.

"Do you want to eat, Aton?" She offered him the food.

He looked at it and said nothing.

"It's safe enough." She ripped a piece out of the meat, chewed it, and swallowed.

"Yes," he said.

She held the meat close to his mouth. It was several days old, but the smell still intoxicated him. He bit into it ravenously.

"Too bad I had to treat you like that." Her tone was calculatedly casual. "But when I found you, you attacked me. In a group like this, any act against me must be punished. Severely, and publicly."

"You took the ax away from me," Aton said as he chewed the meat.

"So?"

"If someone steals from me, they return it."

She shook her head. Deliberately, she moved back and set down the hunk of meat. "You have a lot to learn."

He waited without speaking. He looked at the meat—clearly, a potential reward for good conduct. He looked at Oris's face. Once again her expression was carefully controlled: a mask of indifference.

"No one in my group owns anything," she told him. "No one except me. You understand?"

"I understand. But I don't accept it."

She hit him hard on the side of his jaw. Aton's head jerked back and banged against the stony column behind him. He grunted in pain.

"I chose to let you live," she said. "I can just as easily let you die. We could leave you here for the salamanders to eat. Or I could tell my people to stone you to death. They do whatever I say, without question."

Aton closed his eyes. "Yes."

"All right." She allowed him another bite of the meat. He flinched as he chewed it. His jaw was painful where she had hit him. "It seems to me,

Aton," she went on, "you're an intelligent man. We should both be on the same side. What are these so-called secrets of yours? Maybe we can help each other." She took the lump of meat away again, and set it down.

Aton sighed. "I said what I said so you'd let me live. The truth is, I remember almost nothing. I regained consciousness in that cavern a few minutes before you found me there. Maybe I've got concussion. I must have been in some kind of accident. A few things are starting to come back, but—"

She stood up. He had to crane his neck awkwardly in order to see her face. A tic worked at her cheek for a moment as she glared at him, her eyes dark and fierce. She had seemed rational, but she was not.

"Our god is an evil god," she told him. "Chthon has no mercy. Chthon uses people as he sees fit. Sometimes, he takes over a man's soul, and when that happens, we have to force the evil out."

Aton said nothing.

"Do you know how we force out the evil, Aton?" She squatted in front of him, inches away. Without warning, she punched him hard in the solar plexus.

She watched as Aton vomited up the scraps of food he'd eaten. "Pain, Aton. Pain will cure the evil in your soul." She picked up the bowl, tossed the water into his face, and walked away.

He sat alone, shivering and exhausted. He could surrender his strength, submit to this woman's will, and beg for his own survival. Or, he could defy her and die.

The second choice was self-destruction, but the

first was intolerable. Hate, he told himself; hate would give him the strength he needed to endure and eventually strike back. Yet the hate he expected to find was not there.

His thoughts drifted, and he let them. It was beyond his resources, now, to plan strategically.

He slipped gradually into semiconsciousness, and no longer heard the faint sounds of the river and occasional shouts from convicts fishing downstream. Sleep, of a sort, captured his mind.

With it came dreams; and memories.

CHAPTER 1 _____

It was a different world.

The setting sun was turning the sky crimson and purple as the transit capsule landed gently in the forest glade. The hatch hissed open and Aton stepped out into stillness. He stood and inhaled air rich with the smell of blossoms.

The woman whose name was Malice came out and joined him, her red hair shimmering in the last light from the sky. "You have everything you need?" she asked.

"Yes." He carried only a simple cloth bag containing some basic possessions. This world of Minion, which seemed so enticingly bucolic, was Proscribed— prohibited to outsiders. He had brought nothing with him that would betray his offworld origins.

She raised a metal disk, murmured a command into it, and held it out toward the ship. The silver capsule seemed not to respond at first; then, gradually, it lifted into the air and drifted upward. It gleamed as it rose into sunlight, and then it was gone.

She turned and slipped her arm through his. "Are you ready?"

"To see your home? Yes." Her beauty was even more compelling in reality than it had been in his fantasies during the years he had been searching for her. Deliberately, he looked away.

She parted her lips and shook her long red hair back behind her shoulders. "You're not happy," she said.

He said nothing; there was no point in affirming what she already knew. Like all the women of this world, she possessed sufficient telepathic ability to sense the emotions of anyone near her.

"Walk with me, Aton." She took his arm again, so lightly that he barely felt her fingers on his sleeve. She led him along a path through tall grass, beneath strange dark trees whose velvet-sheened, pink-and-purple blossoms were opening their mouths wide as the sun set.

"It still hurts to know the truth about you," he said. "Even more, about myself." He looked up at the sky. There were two crescent moons, one silver, one pale gold. Stars were beginning to come out, and the air was a warm, gentle caress. "I sometimes used to dream that if I ever found you I would hurt you—*punish* you, for making me so obsessed with you."

She touched his cheek gently with her fingertip, as if the grimness of his expression pleased her. "You may punish me as much and as often as you like. Haven't I already told you so?"

He grimaced. "I'm sickened by my own violence."

"Because you grew up on a different world. But as

I showed you yesterday, you yourself are half Minion. It's natural, for you, to want to hurt the people you care for. I'll show you; you will no longer despise your own anger."

He grunted noncommittally, and stepped around a patch of thorned, bulbous plants, like cacti crowned with clusters of delicate leaves. A small creature stirred suddenly in the undergrowth and Aton heard it scamper to safety. Had he not known better, he would have guessed that human beings had never set foot in this unspoiled landscape.

In fact, he knew, Minion had been colonized for more than three hundred years. She had told him some of the details on their trip here. Originally, the planet had been the site of a scheme to create so-called Minionettes, a female genotype to be cloned from an "ideal woman": beautiful, compliant, responsive to a man's every mood, and virtually immune to the aging process. The experiment had gone horribly wrong, creating grotesque personality disorders that quickly led to the planet's quarantined status. Minionettes were indeed sensitive to a man's thoughts and feelings—but their responses had been inverted. To their telepathic senses, a man's love gave them pain, while his cruelest anger created in them a pure, sensual pleasure.

Aton and Malice reached the top of a low hill. Faintly, in the semidarkness, he could see the shape of a small cabin at the bottom of he next valley. It was surrounded by trees whose pale, feathery leaves dangled like streamers, fluttering silently in the night air. "There's my home," she told him.

Aton glanced at her. She looked exactly the way she had looked when she had first shown herself to him almost twenty years ago. Her beauty was almost more than he could bear.

They walked in silence down the hillside, till they reached the wooden door to the cottage. There, she turned to face him. Her face was almost invisible in the darkness, but her eyes glinted in the moonlight. She was staring up at him expectantly.

He took hold of her bare arms. He hadn't intended to hold her so roughly, but as he felt the softness of her skin, his fingers clenched hard and dug deep. "This is what you want?"

She went limp in his grip. "More."

His fingers tightened further. She gave a cry; but it was of pleasure, not pain.

Aton realized he was suddenly, intensely aroused. He released her and looked away, ashamed to meet her eyes.

"Aton, please. Come inside." She opened the door.

He followed her in, moving woodenly, and waited while she lit a candle. She had not been here for a while; her secret travels had taken her far from Minion. She busied herself around the room, opening the windows, unfolding a clean cover over a simple mattress on a wooden frame.

"I'm sorry it isn't more comfortable," she said. "You must realize, as a Proscribed world, Minion is deprived of trade, and it has few resources of its own. Most homes are even more primitive than mine."

He shook his head. "There's no need to apologize."

In fact, he hardly saw his surroundings. He was staring at her body as she moved to and fro, imagining her naked, and imagining himself inflicting the pain that she claimed she wanted from him.

She lit a second candle, placed it beside the bed, then went to a wood-burning stove beside some shelves mounted on the opposite wall. "Are you hungry? Do you want to eat? I left some dried foods here, and some preserves."

"No." He pictured himself beating her, defacing her beauty. The idea sickened him, yet it was an aphrodisiac.

Her telepathic sense told her what he was feeling. She sat down on the edge of the bed and reached behind her neck to unbutton her dress. As she arched her back, her breasts pushed up provocatively. She smiled, enjoying the torment she roused in him.

He stood motionless while she took off her clothes. When she was naked, she walked over to him. Her physical presence was a drug; for years he had fantasized having her before him as she was now.

But he made no move to touch her. "You know, I thought that if I tracked you down, I could resolve the conflict inside myself, and be free. But now I can see that it doesn't work that way. Since finding you, in the last two days, the obsession has grown even stronger."

"It's a part of you," she told him softly. "You can never find contentment by trying to escape from your own self." She picked up something from a low table beside her bed. "Here." She handed it to him. "This will help."

Dumbly, Aton took it from her. It was a short, tightly braided leather whip.

She lay down on the bed, displaying her nakedness to him. "Come to me, Aton. Hurt me."

CHAPTER 2 _____

Morning sunlight splashed across the bedcover as if to wash away the residues of the night. Aton lay watching Malice as she moved to and fro, humming to herself, setting dishes on the table by the window. She had woken several hours earlier and slipped out to buy food from a nearby farm. Now there was wood crackling in the stove, fat sizzling in a pan. It was a scene of simple domesticity—and it was a lie.

She paused and smiled at him. It was the bright-eyed, sensual smile of a woman looking at her lover—and that, too, was a lie.

The truth was a parody of love. Last night he had done what she asked. He had vented years of frustration and rage, had beaten her savagely, and the more abuse he had inflicted, the more ecstatic she had become. Her appetite was endless and her skin seemed almost immune to bruising or abrasion. She was not, of course, a normal woman; she was a genetic oddity, descended from a flawed experiment. But during the night, he had forgotten her origins and his own. His awareness had contracted until he experienced nothing beyond the eroticism of brutality.

"Are you hungry, Aton?" She finished slicing purplish native vegetables on a cutting board, placed a fresh loaf of peasant bread on the table, then started scrambling fresh eggs from chickens whose ancestors had been imported from Old Earth.

He sat up without answering, swung his legs over the side of the bed, and quickly pulled on his clothes. He glimpsed himself in a small mirror hanging on the opposite wall: clear blue eyes, a square jaw gray with a day's beard, a brooding mouth, untidy auburn hair. The sight did not please him.

She stirred the eggs in the pan and added the vegetables around them. Aton pulled his shoes on and stepped outside. The sun was already warm. He squinted into the cloudless sky, then surveyed the lush vegetation that crowded around the cabin. It was disconcerting for him to remember that he was half Minion; that this world was as much his home as the planet Hvee, where he had spent his childhood.

He found a rain barrel near the door, splashed his face with water, and dried it on his sleeve. He walked back into the cabin and sat down at the table. She placed food before him and sat opposite, once again smiling shyly at him.

He ate in silence. The food was delicately spiced and the bread was warm and fragrant, with a crisp crust. After years of eating concentrates in interstellar flight, the meal should have been a special pleasure. Yet he hardly tasted it.

Her smile faltered. "You're not pleased with me," she said in a small voice.

He cleaned his plate with another slice of bread, and said nothing.

"You're still angry?"

He stopped. "Yes, I'm angry. I'm angry with myself, for being the way I am, and with you, for tempting me with my own perversion."

She half closed her eyes, as if sampling a perfume. "I feel your anger. It's hard and bright and cruel."

He seized her wrist. "Haven't you had enough?"

She shook her head. "Never enough."

He twined his fingers in her long red hair, twisted his wrist, and jerked her head back so that she was forced to look up at him. Quickly, with his other hand, he slapped her face. The blow was severe. She gave a little cry and closed her eyes. "Yes," she whispered.

Despite himself, Aton felt passion building again. It would be an endless cycle: He hated her for the morbid desires she provoked. She became aroused by his hate, and provoked him still more.

She made him feel like a freak, unfit for normal society. No wonder the planet Minion had been Proscribed. Its women carried seeds of insanity.

"I hate you," he told her. "I truly do."

She smiled radiantly. "I know."

He raised his hand to hit her again, but this time the blow never fell. He was distracted by a movement outside the window.

"What is it?" she asked, sensing the change in him.

"People." Three men dressed in crude brown uniforms and leather helmets were gradually coming into view through the trees.

Malice peered out, then quickly motioned Aton to step back. "The king's guard," she said softly.

"Are they coming here?"

"There's nowhere else they could be going. No one lives nearby."

"But how could they know you're back on Minion?"

She shook her head. "They shouldn't be aware that I ever left. I took great care to conceal my comings and goings; you know the penalties." Her sensual submissiveness had vanished. She seemed suddenly cool and rational. "You must hide," she told him. "Quickly. Under the bed; that's the only place. They're probably on some routine business, and they have no reason to suspect that an offworlder is here. It's best if they don't question you; you don't look like most Minion men."

He hesitated, sensing that she was not telling him the whole truth. "I don't want to—"

"Do as I say!"

Strange to be suddenly obeying her commands. But this was her world, not his. He lay down on the bare boards and eased himself under the wooden frame of the bed. There was barely enough room. She draped the bedcover so that it concealed him.

He could see nothing from his hiding place, but he heard Malice taking the dishes from the table, for two plates would have been obvious evidence that she was not alone.

There was a peremptory knock on the door. Aton heard the hinges creak as Malice opened it.

Heavy boots stamped into the little room. A scroll of parchment rustled. "You are the woman, name of

Malice." It was a statement, not an inquiry. They didn't wait for her to answer. "You dwell here alone."

"That's true," she said. "Although—"

"Quiet," said another, older voice.

"It is my duty to read to you paragraph three of the marriage laws of this kingdom," the first voice droned on, "which states: any woman of childbearing ability who lacks a husband and also lacks a son to take his place shall be allowed a period not exceeding five Earth standard years in which to remarry, at the end of such period, *if* she remains unwed, she shall submit herself to the King's Initiations, at a time and place to be chosen at His Majesty's discretion." The scroll rustled again as he put it away.

"I am well aware of the law," she said. There was a note of defiance in her voice that he hadn't heard before. Evidently, a Minionette was not submissive to all men, only to her partner. Aton wished he had had more than just two days to learn about her. He had no idea what an "initiation" entailed. He could reveal himself—perhaps confront the guards, even attempt to run with her. But her capsule was in a high orbit; it would take an hour to call it down. And even if they did manage to escape, anyone who saw or deduced what had happened could report it to the authorities, and word would be broadcast from the transmitter that was maintained on Minion by the Quarantine Department of the Interstellar Federation.

"All right, come with us," said the voice.

"Now?"

"Yes, now. The Initiations are today, woman.

Where've you been? We came to give you the official notice a week back."

"I was away," she answered. "In another village. I've—found a new mate."

There was a pause. "What's his name?"

"He lives a day's walk from here. He—"

"You have proof?"

"I am an innocent citizen," she said. "If I'm innocent of a crime, why should I have to prove it?"

"We're wasting time," said another voice. "Put the cuffs on her."

"No!" Her voice was shrill.

There was the sound of a struggle, then the clicking of a metal lock. A man exclaimed in anger. "Bitch! She bit me."

Aton heard another guard move forward. There was the sound of a fist hitting flesh. Malice tumbled down onto the floor beside the bed. If the cover had not been draped over his hiding place, Aton would have been face-to-face with her.

"Leave off," said the older voice. "She'll get more than enough of that this afternoon."

There was rough laughter then, and they dragged Malice up off the floor.

Before they did so, however, her hand slid surreptitiously under the bed, almost touching Aton. When her fingers withdrew, they left behind the silver disk that could call her ship down from the sky.

The door of the cabin creaked open, the heavy footsteps departed, and Aton was alone.

After waiting a couple of seconds to be certain that no one was still in the room, he crawled out. He looked at the disk and wondered for a moment if she expected him to use the ship to rescue her. No; she was telling him to take it and save himself.

He peered cautiously out of the window and saw the soldiers marching her off through the trees, with her wrists handcuffed behind her. He stood and watched, and he did nothing.

Finally, they disappeared from view. Aton groaned, ran his fingers through his hair, and sat down heavily on the bed. He stared at the mattress, where she had yielded to him during the night.

He cursed under his breath, thrust the disk angrily into his pocket, and strode out of the cabin. The four soldiers had not yet gone far, and it should be easy enough to track them through the rough terrain without being noticed.

He started after them.

chapter iii _____

A hand touched his shoulder. He woke slowly to cold rock and dripping water, aching limbs and an empty stomach. He was sitting where Oris had left him, tied to the big stalagmite on the floor of the cave. He blinked in the claustrophobic semidarkness. A woman was squatting in front of him, shaking him awake.

"Malice," he murmured, still seeing dream images of the Minionette. But that had been decades ago, light-years distant. He was on Chthon, now. He groaned softly.

The woman pressed her finger to his lips. "Quiet," she whispered to him. "Everyone's asleep."

Aton focused on her. She was small with pointed features, a thin face, hair cropped short, a scar across her cheek. She glanced nervously to either side, and edged closer. "It was wrong what they did to you." She nodded, as if agreeing with what she had just said. "Don't tell Oris I said so, but it was wrong."

Aton grunted noncommittally. He tried to move his arms, and winced. He realized he must have been sitting slumped in this position, unconscious, for several hours.

"You okay?" the woman whispered.

"They tied my wrists too tight. I can't feel my arms anymore."

"Oh." She didn't make any move to help him. "Oris says you're evil," she went on. She scratched her thin belly, under her clothes. "Says you're possessed."

"I'm no better or worse than anyone else."

She seemed to think about that. "But it was spooky finding you in that little cave, like a *sign* or something. Look, my name's Elen. I come here to see if you need anything. I don't like to see people suffer when they done nothing wrong."

"Then do something about my wrists," Aton told her.

She blinked. She seemed a mess of nervous mannerisms. "If I do, you better not try anything. You try anything, and I'll scream. They'll all come running, kill you most likely."

"I understand that."

"All right, then." She moved silently, like a shadow. He felt her fingers tugging at the knots holding his wrists, and then his arms were free.

Aton doubled forward, hugging himself. He gasped as blood surged into the veins of his hands, making them tingle and throb.

Elen reappeared in front of him. "You got to do things for me now." She squatted down in front of him. "That's only fair. Right?"

Aton saw the lump of meat that Oris had left lying on the ground. His hands were burning and his muscles were stiff, but he was able to pick up the meat and hold it. He took a big bite. "What do you want?" He started untying his ankles while he ate.

She glanced either side, then moved closer again. "You said like you know secrets. About Chthon."

He swallowed the mouthful and took another. "I just said that to save my neck."

"You mean it wasn't true?" She looked childishly disappointed.

He sighed. "I've lost most of my memories. I don't know exactly where I am, or what happened to me."

"Oh." She rubbed her nose with a thin, grimy hand, then chewed on her knuckle, watching him doubtfully.

He shrugged. "Take it or leave it."

"You sure remember how to fight. You had Oris up against the wall, when we found you."

"I can look after myself." He devoured the rest of the meat, saw a deep puddle nearby, and scooped the water in his hands. It tasted metallic but was drinkable.

"Maybe you can look after me, too." She gave him a gap-toothed grin.

He glanced down at her body, scrawny beneath the shapeless convict garb. He grunted. "Perhaps."

She touched his arm, then his chest. "You're strong. Why'd you get sent here to Chthon, anyhow? You kill some people or something?"

He shook his head. "No. Although, I suppose it's possible. There was one woman—" He paused, haunted by a sudden mental image of Malice, his hands around her neck, rage surging through him. A memory, or a fantasy; it was impossible to tell.

"You maybe killed your girlfriend?"

He laughed without humor. "She wasn't my girlfriend. More my nemesis."

"Love-hate, huh?"

"Sometimes I wonder if there's a difference." But his memory-dream of Malice had no relevance here. He shut the thoughts away. "So you and your people are on the hard trek. Searching for a way out."

"Yeah. You going to help us find it?"

"I don't know. I really don't know anything."

"All right, Elen. That's enough." It was Oris's voice.

Aton looked up, startled. Oris was standing a few feet away with her hands on her hips, Jacko beside her.

Elen scrambled away from Aton. She tugged at Oris's sleeve. "Was it the way you wanted? I did as good as I could, didn't I? You heard me, I did just what you said. I tried to get him to talk to me."

"You did fine," said Oris. "Go back to the camp. Tell everyone to get ready to move on."

"Okay. I'll do that. Whatever you say." She ran off, disappearing among the pillars of rock.

Aton got to his feet. "I should have guessed it was a setup." He remembered how it had felt to pin Oris's body against the wall in the small cavern, when he'd been trying to recapture his ax from her. He flexed his fingers, wondering if he'd ever get a chance to do more. He imagined having power over her, taking revenge for the way she had deceived and abused him.

She seemed to sense his thoughts. She showed no fear, but kept her distance from him. "Jacko, tie his wrists again."

The big man swaggered forward. He stooped to pick up the length of cloth that Elen had untied, then reached for Aton's arm.

Aton turned quickly and drove his elbow deep into the man's stomach. Jacko gasped and doubled forward. Aton chopped his fat neck, hard. Jacko lurched, almost losing his balance. Aton kicked the side of his knee, and Jacko's leg went out from under him. He fell sprawling on his stomach.

Aton jammed his foot on the side of Jacko's throat, holding him down. He seized a heavy rock and raised it, aiming for Jacko's head. He glanced at Oris.

"Go ahead," Oris said, her dark eyes mocking him. "Kill him. Then what are you going to do? Run away? Or take on all the rest of us, too?"

Aton paused. Again, he remembered: it was impossible to survive in Chthon alone. He grimaced, tossed the rock aside, and stepped back. Jacko scrambled up, red-faced, a vein standing out on his forehead.

"I don't like being deceived," Aton said to Oris. "I don't like being manipulated."

"It makes no difference what you like or don't like." She gestured peremptorily. "Turn around and put your hands behind your back."

Aton swallowed hard, holding back his anger. He did as she said and waited in silence while Jacko lashed his wrists cruelly tight.

"You'll walk with us," Oris told Aton, "until I decide what to do with you. Jacko, keep an eye on him." She turned on her heel and strode away.

"Scum," said Jacko. He spat in Aton's face, then grabbed him by the hair. "This way, scum." He dragged Aton after him.

The march was long and painful. The rock was rough under Aton's bare feet, and his muscles protested against the constant exertion. Picking his way through rock-strewn caverns and tunnels, with his arms tied behind him, it was hard to keep his balance. Each time he slipped or stumbled Jacko grabbed him roughly, jerked him upright, and kicked him forward.

"Did Oris tell you to do that, or is it just your way of enjoying yourself?" Aton snapped at the big man.

"Oris got nothing to do with it, scum." He pushed Aton in the back, sending him staggering forward along the narrow passageway they were in.

"Seems to me Oris has a lot to do with it," Aton said. "Seems she's always bossing someone around. You, especially."

"Shut your mouth, scum. You got no right to say nothing about her. Understand?"

Aton paused. He turned and examined Jacko's grimy bearded face. "Are you jealous? Is that it? You know, maybe she let me live, back there, because she likes the look of me. Come to think of it, she could be keeping me around in case something happens to you."

Jacko's face twitched. He bared his teeth, grabbed

Aton by the throat, and threw him hard against the wall. "All right, you asked for it."

"Hey, now, break it up." The man who'd been marching behind them laid his hand on Jacko's shoulder and tried to put himself between the two of them. "There's no time for fighting."

"Keep out of this, Votnik."

"We need to keep moving, Jacko. What's more important, a fistfight, or getting out of here alive? Eh?" He had a bushy black beard, a bald head, and a wide, fleshy, friendly face. His body looked soft and he had a paunch. He seemed the type who might have spent much of his life eating well and drinking heavily, before committing some high-level white-collar crime serious enough to get him banished to Chthon.

Jacko stared at the man. "There's no way I'm going to take whatever this scum feels like calling me."

"Look, I'll walk with him for a while," said Votnik.

"What's the trouble back there?" Oris's voice echoed along the tunnel from up ahead.

"No trouble," Votnik shouted back to her. "But I'll look after your prisoner for an hour or two. How's that sound?"

"You do whatever you want. Just keep moving."

Jacko grunted in disgust. He turned away from Aton, pushed past him, and ambled on up the tunnel.

Aton nodded to Votnik. "Thanks," he said.

"My pleasure. Seems to me, though, you could take some lessons in making friends."

Aton stared at Jacko's broad shoulders, a few paces

ahead. "Some people I don't regard as fit for human company, let alone friendship."

Votnik smiled. The plump flesh bunched up around his small, sharp eyes. "Now that's plain talk. And I've always said as I respect an honest man. But there's such a thing as live and let live. Did you ever hear of that?"

"Yes. Mainly from people who didn't want to fight for anything they believed in."

Votnik chuckled as if Aton had told him a joke. "Man of principle, eh?" He eyed Aton speculatively. "I've always said as I admire a man of principle. Myself, I'd rather live an easy life on friendly terms than fight for a principle. What's so important that it's worth fighting for?"

"Independence," Aton told him.

"Oh. Now that's unfortunate. You'll find none of that here, friend. The only people Oris trusts are the ones who follow orders."

"I've noticed."

Votnik glanced at Aton's wrists tied behind him. "Why yes indeed, so you have."

The two of them walked in silence for a few minutes, following Jacko and a dozen other convicts ahead, the rest trudging along behind. "So where are you from?" Votnik asked. "If you don't mind my inquiring."

"That depends on whether it's your question, or whether Oris told you to ask it."

Votnik shrugged. "The fact is, my friend, we'd all like to know some more about you."

"So far as I can remember," Aton told him, "I was born on the planet Hvee."

"Can't say I've heard of it. Undeveloped, is it?"

"I . . . think so. I seem to remember farmland."

"Well, I was a city boy, myself; happiest under a dome. Went into banking. Still, I've always said as I respect a man with roots in the soil. Yes indeed. Barry Votnik's the name. You?"

"Aton Five."

Votnik tilted his head to one side. "Five? What sort of name's that?"

"On my home world, a family's status was measured by its number."

"Which makes you part of the aristocracy, eh?" Votnik chuckled, making his double chins wobble. His eyes didn't change, though; they studied Aton shrewdly. "So it seems there's some things you can remember after all, Mr. Five."

Aton nodded. "Some of my childhood has come back to me. But I still don't know how I came to be here in Chthon."

"Too bad, too bad." Votnik paused. "And I suppose you wouldn't remember anything about how to find a way out of it, either."

"Anyone who knew that," said Aton, "would no longer be here."

Yet Votnik's question had triggered another memory. Aton saw himself emerging from the labyrinth into the bright sunlight of a pastoral paradise after years trapped underground. Behind him, a trail of death: comrades on his own hard trek who had succumbed to disease and predators. Ahead of him, the promise of freedom.

Suddenly he remembered again the words Bedeker had spoken, when he had woken in the small cavern: "You have returned to Chthon."

The implication was obvious. In order to *return* to this prison, in the past he must have found a way to leave it.

"Something on your mind?" Votnik inquired.

"Nothing." Aton shook his head. "Nothing at all."

chapter iv _____

They marched for two hours more. Each time a passageway branched, Oris took the path that sloped upward. Gradually the air became warmer and the glowing lichen grew more prolifically, so that the caves became progressively brighter.

They rested, finally, in a smooth-walled chamber that might once have been a gas bubble in Chthon's volcanic crust. The convicts ranged themselves around the bowl-shaped floor and shared meager rations of dried meat and fish. A water skin was passed from hand to hand, and Oris allowed Votnik to untie Aton's wrists so that he could take his share.

Most of the convicts looked exhausted. Some nursed ugly wet blisters on their feet; others simply slumped against the rock walls with their eyes closed. Aton guessed that the group had been marching for many weeks, although time was almost impossible to gauge in this world without day or night.

"Getting low on food," Jacko remarked. He glanced at Aton. "And now we got another mouth to feed."

"He stays with us," Oris said flatly.

"Man's a troublemaker," Jacko persisted. "You seen that yourself."

Several of the others looked at Aton. It was hard to tell what was going on in their minds. "He don't talk much," said a thin, weasel-faced man whom Aton had learned was named Snyder. "I don't trust a fella who don't talk. Ain't natural."

"Until I decide if he's useful or not, he stays with us," Oris repeated. She stared at each of them in turn, inviting any of them to defy her authority.

"Easy, easy," said Votnik. "Seems to me, a man's innocent till he's proved guilty."

"It seems to me," Aton said carefully, "that my being here isn't the real problem. The real problem is that people are tired and hungry, there isn't enough food, and there's still no hope of finding a way out. That's enough to make everyone short-tempered."

"Man's got a point," said Votnik.

"But you'd think this would be good hunting territory," Aton went on. "There's plenty of lichen here. It's strange we haven't seen any trace of animals."

"Creatures don't like it where it's bright," said Jacko.

"But lichen must be their primary source of food. The more lichen, the more wildlife."

"Who told you that?" Oris asked, watching him closely.

Aton shrugged. "No one. It's logical deduction. Any fool can see—"

"Watch your mouth, you!" Jacko lumbered to his feet.

Aton was about to reply, but a faint tremor in the

rock distracted him. No one else seemed to have felt it, but he knew instinctively what it was. Images came to him of his past life on Chthon, hunting to stay alive.

He stood up slowly, facing Jacko. Talk, he realized, would take too long. He darted forward, snatched Jacko's knife from its sheath, jumped to one side before the big man could react, and ran out of the chamber, down a steeply sloping tunnel. Behind him he heard confused shouts, then footsteps coming after him. But his ears were tuned to the faint thrumming from passageways ahead.

Aton caught a whiff of animal odor. The tunnel divided and he took the fork that continued sloping down. It closed in around him and he ran doubled over, his breath rasping loud in the confined space. He leaped across a deep fissure, ducked an overhang, and dived down another tunnel, using reflexes learned long ago and never forgotten. He sensed that the tube he was in would curve around, and it did, bringing him out ahead of his prey.

He emerged at an intersection almost face-to-face with a glowmole. It was a large one, almost filling the tube it was in. It sensed Aton ahead of it more by smell than by its dim eyesight. It stopped in its tracks and attempted to turn, then realized the tunnel was too narrow. It tried to back away, but couldn't move fast enough. Aton dived forward and wrapped his arm around the creature's thick neck.

Its hide was rough and spiky, dangerous if you touched it carelessly. Memories flooded into Aton's mind, of other hunts, and times he had actually tamed the creatures and ridden them. But no time to think of that now. The glowmole thrashed under him and tried to claw him off. Aton felt under the creature's throat, knowing where to find the sensitive spot. He dug the knife deep.

The animal made a keening noise. Its taloned feet scrabbled at the floor of the tunnel, chipping stone. Its blood gushed out.

Aton slid off and stepped back as the creature writhed and fell on its side. He scrambled up the passageway, spattered by the red tide. He felt a moment of regret, watching the glowmole succumb to its wound; it was a herbivore, harmless unless provoked.

He heard the sound of running feet and turned quickly. Several of the convicts were coming down the tunnel toward him. They stopped when they saw him by the animal, the knife still in his hand. The stench of its blood was strong in the narrow tunnel as it thrashed feebly in its own blood.

"Out of the way." It was Oris, pushing past the men. She emerged in front of Aton and saw the body of the glowmole.

"I heard it while we were talking," Aton said. He felt animal blood trickling down his cheek, and wiped it aside. "I noticed tremors in the rock. There was no time to explain."

"Bullshit," said Jacko. "There ain't no way he could've heard—"

"Quiet," Oris snapped at him. "You men, start cutting up the meat. Aton, give Jacko his knife."

Aton paused as if considering whether to obey. Finally, he surrendered the blade.

"Snyder, Votnik, Rogers, Gwinnie—after you cut the meat, carry it back to the chamber we were in, and clean it and bag it." She turned to Aton. "I want you to come with me."

He followed her back up the tunnel, and into the next passageway that would take them back the way they had come. "I think you're making a mistake," he told Oris.

She stopped and turned. "What?"

"I may be wrong. But killing the mole—it made me remember. This whole section of Chthon feels familiar."

She eyed him dubiously. "Meaning what?"

"I used to live down here. There was a large cavern, a river, plants that grew there. It was quite— idyllic. If we found that place, your people could rest and recuperate. It seems to me that everyone needs that. You'll never make it if you keep on the way you are."

She pointed her finger at his chest. "Listen. When we started out on the hard trek, there were some men in the group who didn't think a woman was fit to lead it. They thought they could do a better job." She shook her head. "None of them survived."

"What happened to them?"

"They're gone. Just remember, I'm the one the people trust, and I'm the one who's held the group together, through all the suffering, all the hardship."

"And I'm the one who just killed enough meat to

feed you all for the next week. No one else even heard the glowmole."

"True. But so far as I'm concerned, that just makes you more dangerous." She eyed his body, smeared with blood. She seemed to reach a decision. "All right, this paradise you're talking about. Let's suppose I believe you. How close is it?"

"I can't be certain."

"Show me."

He frowned in surprise. "Alone?"

"You won't try to harm me. My people would kill you for it. Anyway, if we're going on a fool's errand, I'd rather do it privately."

Aton nodded. "You mean, if we find something, you'll take the credit. And if we don't, you say nothing. And either way, no one sees *you* following *me*."

She took a deep breath, trying to ignore his provocation. "Just show me where it is," she snapped at him.

"All right," Aton agreed. He turned and surveyed the two tunnels branching away from where he stood. "It seems to me we should head this way."

For a few minutes they walked in silence. He heard her immediately behind him, tense and alert. At first, Aton felt sure he recognized the geometry of his surroundings. But as he walked further, the feeling of certainty faded.

Finally, he had to admit he was lost. He stopped in a small chamber where water trickled down one wall, formed a wide, shallow puddle, and flowed away along yet another tunnel. "I don't recognize this at all," he said.

"Another lapse of memory?"

Aton didn't answer. He was searching his mind for clues, and finding nothing.

"Frankly, your whole story sounded ridiculous." She gave him a careful, calculating look. "But while you're here, where there's water, you might as well wash yourself. You're covered in blood."

Aton had felt it congealing on his face and hands, forming a thick crust. He moved to the puddle, squatted down, and rubbed the water over his skin. He glanced up at Oris, and found her still watching him. Something about her manner had changed. Aton moved carefully, alert for any sign of aggression on her part.

"It's on your tunic, too," she told him.

He stripped the garment off and rinsed it as well as he could. As he started to pull it on again, she strode across and grabbed it out of his hands.

He stood up quickly.

She took his wrist. Slowly, she guided it to her breast. She pressed his hand against her, till he felt the hardness of her nipple through the cloth.

She ran her other hand down his chest, across his belly, and lower. She touched him insistently. Gradually, of its own accord, Aton felt his body beginning to respond.

She gave him a thin smile. "You find me desirable."

"In a purely physical sense."

She punched him in the belly, hard. He fell back,

then went into a crouch, ready to throw himself at her.

She shook her head. "You're forgetting what happens to you if anything happens to me."

Slowly, Aton willed the tension out of his muscles, controlling his anger with difficulty.

She stripped off her own tunic, exposing her body. She was statuesque and well muscled, but no less feminine for it. Her waist was slim and flat, her breasts were high and firm. She glanced down at herself, as if knowing she looked desirable. Then she moved toward Aton. She took his head between her hands and guided it to her breasts. "Kiss my body," she told him.

He saw himself seizing her, throwing her on the floor, punishing her in a frenzy of revenge. But she was right: so long as her people were loyal to her, and he was partly dependent on them for survival, his position was helpless.

Hating her, he did what he was told. After a while he managed to shut off conscious thought and immerse himself in simple animal sensations. The musky smell of her closed around him.

She sank down slowly onto the floor. "Good," she told him. Her eyes were bright; clearly, it aroused her to dominate him. She pushed his head lower. "More," she told him.

After a few minutes, she nudged him onto his back and lowered herself over him. She started moving insistently, looking down at him. She traced the line of the wound in his chest that she had made with the ax blade. "I hurt you there," she said, half to herself.

"Yes."

She fell forward with her hands on his shoulders, holding him down on the floor. "I knew when we found you, I had to have you. But on my terms, not yours."

He clenched his jaw. He said nothing.

She grabbed him by the hair and banged his head on the rocky floor of the cave. "You'll learn to obey me."

But then she froze. She turned her head quickly, staring toward the passageway that led into this little chamber.

Aton was instantly alert. "What is it?" he whispered.

"I don't know. Maybe nothing."

"Jacko?"

She shook her head. Slowly, silently, she lifted herself off him, grabbed her tunic, and pulled it on.

Aton rolled over, found his own wet garment, and struggled into it. "What did you hear?"

"There!" she whispered. That time, he heard it too: a faint shuffling, scraping sound. He looked around quickly for anything that would serve as a weapon, saw a rock the size of his fist, and reached for it.

Suddenly a huge shadowy form was in the chamber. Oris screamed and lunged at it. It threw her aside. She hit the wall, rebounded, and splashed into the puddle on the floor.

Then the creature was on him. Talons grabbed his arms. Foul breath enveloped him. Aton hurled the rock where he guessed the thing's eye might be, then struck out with his fist. There was a roar of anger.

Curved teeth gleamed in the dim green light. Something hard struck the side of his head.

His vision fragmented. Sounds receded. He spiraled among ghost replicas of the cave and heard himself groaning as if from a great distance. Hallucinatory images flowered before him: he saw the cave, saw the cave embedded in the planet, saw the planet turning through space. But space was white, a glaring light that burned his eyes, and the stars were black dots pinwheeling around him.

The whiteness faded into green—but it was not the lichen green of Chthon.

CHAPTER 3 _____

He moved cautiously through thick vegetation, following a narrow path overgrown with purple grass and flowering weeds. Dark green foliage hung from trees all around, festooned with exotic blossoms that trembled in the gentle breeze. Insects hummed in the fragrant air.

The guards escorting Malice were a short distance ahead. Aton considered creeping closer and trying to take her from them. He would have the advantage of surprise, and he doubted these simple peasants would be any match for the fighting skills he had learned in his youth on the high-gravity world of Hvee. Yet there were three of them, armed with swords, while Aton possessed no weapon of any kind.

After slightly more than a mile the narrow path emerged from under the trees and joined a cart track. Aton crouched behind a thicket of thorn bushes and watched the guards start along the track to the west, marching Malice with them. Cautiously, he followed, keeping well back.

The track was deeply rutted, but the mud had been baked dry by the sun. Evidently Minion's rainy season had ended some time ago. Aton wished he knew more about the planet. All he had to go on were the few facts that Malice had mentioned during the past two days.

He reached the crest of a hill. Ahead, nestling in a shallow valley, was a village of mud huts with thatched roofs. The guards were taking her toward it. Aton saw the sunlight gleaming on her bright red hair, and felt a twist of emotion that he found hard to name. Reluctantly, he followed them.

The village smelled of mud and dung. The crude little huts were spaced at intervals along the cart track with horses outside them, tethered amid swarms of flies.

A woman was walking toward Aton, staggering under the weight of two enormous leather buckets of water suspended from a wooden yoke across her shoulders. Her body was concealed in a long toga, and a veil hid most of her face; but when a momentary breeze blew the veil aside, Aton glimpsed her features clearly. Her resemblance to Malice was eerie, yet he realized it was inevitable: all females on Minion were descended from the same genetically engineered stock, designed to breed true.

Behind her was a small gnomelike man with a ferocious beard. He was naked except for a loincloth and carried a pointed stick. "Goddamned lazy bitch!" he yelled. "I should put *you* in the Initiations. Come on, damn it!"

He swung the stick and dealt the woman a blow across the backs of her thighs. She stumbled, almost dropping her burden. Aton heard her gasp—but behind her veil, she smiled.

The little man noticed Aton and frowned as if he didn't like what he saw. "Something you want, mister?"

"No. I didn't mean to stare."

"From the South Country, are you?"

Aton shrugged. "That's right."

"Man your size, couldn't hardly be from anyplace else. Come to watch the Initiations?"

Aton nodded. "Although I'm not sure what—"

The little man chuckled. "Yes, you're big, but I can see you're young. First time for you, eh? Well, the single women are put before the King, and he tests 'em, out in the village square, and those that are fit, he takes to the palace, and those that aren't—" He grinned nastily. "It's something to see, all right. Damn it, though, I'll miss it myself if this whore doesn't get to work." He whirled around and smacked his stick hard across her shins. "Did I tell you to stand there listening?"

"No, master." Her voice was gentle and melodic.

"Then get that water home, and heat it so's I can wash. Do you hear me?" He took careful aim, then savagely jabbed the pointed end of the stick into her flank.

"Yes, master." She said it with a little sigh of pleasure as she staggered on along the track.

"Never gets enough, that one." The little man winked at Aton. "Wears me out, I'm telling you." He strutted away, following the woman and cursing her freely.

Aton closed his eyes for a moment, overwhelmed with self-loathing. Yet wasn't that why he had asked Malice to bring him to Minion? He had wanted to know the whole truth so he could come to terms with it. No matter how unpleasant it was, it had to be better than the limbo of ignorance he had endured for most of his life.

Nearer the center of the village he found a barn where horses and cattle were being traded, and a ramshackle general store. Men were chatting to one another, veiled women were standing docilely with their heads bowed, and children were playing in the dirt. Aton noticed that all the children were male, and remembered what Malice had told him while they were traveling to Minion in her transit capsule. On this world, men seldom lived past the age of seventy, but women could expect to survive for two centuries. The child that a woman had with her first husband was always male, so that as the husband grew older and died, the child could replace him as the woman's new husband. He, in turn, would give her a son, who would take *his* place; and so on, until the woman neared the end of her life expectancy. Only then would she give birth to a daughter, to replace herself.

People were moving into a central area paved with rough-hewn stone. Aton followed them. All the Minion men were smaller than himself—smaller, in many cases, than their women. He felt uncomfortably conspicuous, although the hand-woven clothes that Malice had given him were typical of the garments worn by the male villagers, and helped him to blend in. He hunched his shoulders and stayed at the edge of the crowd.

Most of the men carried sticks or clubs and herded the women like animals, cursing them and beating them at the slightest provocation. Several led their wives on ropes like dog leashes, and one who was particularly scrawny sat on his woman's shoulders, goading her with metal spurs attached to his sandals. Yet there were no cries of distress from the veiled women, nor even a voice raised in complaint. To a Minionette, her husband's hate was truly the love on which she thrived. When Aton glimpsed the faces of the women who were most savagely abused, they were the ones who looked most radiantly fulfilled.

The Minion side of his nature reacted with voyeuristic fascination. To own one of these ageless creatures and treat her as a slave, abusing her as he wished—the idea roused sinister longings. At the same time, he saw the cost it would entail. He would be able to express only hate, never love. If what Malice had told him was true, love could cause pain, injury, even death, when experienced by the semitelepathic senses of a Minionette.

His thoughts were interrupted by a crude blast on a trumpet. A wooden platform had been erected at the opposite side of the square, and one of the King's guards was standing in the center of it.

The villagers pressed forward, a ragged crowd of perhaps two hundred. The guard stamped the heel of his boot three times on the wooden stage. "All kneel for His Majesty!" He blew another trumpet blast, turned to the right, and dropped to one knee himself, bowing his head.

The crowd of villagers got down on their knees and Aton did the same. He saw a sedan chair moving toward the platform, carried on the shoulders of four beautiful Minionettes in chains. The chair was crusted in fake gems and gold paint and was upholstered in faded red velvet. Seated in it was a grossly fat little man, barely taller than a dwarf, dressed in elaborately embroidered satin robes and a tarnished silver crown. His face was as puffed up as his body, to the point where his eyes were tiny slits above cheeks like apples. A scraggly beard rimmed a mouth like a beak. His features were contorted in a furious scowl.

"All hail His Majesty!" shouted the guard.

"All hail," the crowd echoed dutifully.

The four women carried the chair up onto the stage. They set it down and stepped back, their eyes downcast. The King beckoned to the guard and pointed to one of the women whose grip had faltered noticeably at one point, making the chair lurch.

The guard nodded briefly, walked over, and hit her in the face. She staggered and fell on her back. The guard took a pace forward and kicked her in the stomach, rolling her off the stage, onto the ground below.

The King turned to the crowd and grinned, exposing hideously decayed teeth. Many of the men in the audience applauded, and so did the women.

Aton turned away, feeling sickened. Yet he couldn't leave. If nothing else, he had to know what was going to happen here to Malice.

The King lounged back in his chair. "All rise," he said to the villagers, and dutifully they got back up onto their feet. "Bring 'em on," he told his guard.

The man bowed perfunctorily. "For the pleasure of Your Majesty: Woman by name of Hate. Woman by name of Anger. Woman by name of Malice." As he spoke, five more guards led the women onto the opposite side of the platform.

Aton was less than a hundred feet away; he saw her clearly, red-haired and green-eyed like the others, yet unique. Her clothes were torn, but she stood straight and proud as if she refused to acknowledge the peasants around her.

She looked out over the heads of the crowd and for a moment, her eyes met his. She stiffened with the shock of recognition. Her lips parted in dismay. She gave her head a little shake, as if to tell him he shouldn't be there—he should have fled and saved himself.

But the King was speaking. "That one." He pointed to Malice. "She looks fit enough."

The guards grabbed her and dragged her to a massive wooden post in the center of the platform.

The King nodded approvingly. "String her up. Bring on the Initiator."

CHAPTER 4 _____

Aton felt light-headed, helplessly watching the scene unfold in front of him. The Initiator walked onto the platform, naked from the waist up, wearing heavy gauntlets. His torso was brawny by Minion standards. His head was hidden under a black hood.

He shouted an instruction to the guards. They removed the shackles from Malice's wrists, brought her hands in front of her, and tied them to one end of a long piece of rope. She stood as straight and proud as ever, refusing to look any of them in the eye.

The other end of the rope was threaded through a shackle at the top of the tall wooden post in the center of the platform. The guards pulled on the free end of the rope, drawing it through the shackle till it tightened, dragging Malice's hands above her head.

They continued hauling on the rope. Her arms were stretched up, higher and higher still, till she was forced to stand on tiptoe. The men paused in their work as if enjoying the sight of her helpless in front of them. Then they pulled the rope some more so that it lifted her off her feet. She hung suspended by her wrists, her toes dangling above the wooden platform.

The Initiator barked another instruction, and the guards secured the free end of the rope to a metal bolt set in one side of the post.

The Initiator moved forward. He took a knife from a sheath at his hip and started slicing Malice's clothes off her. He worked quickly and carelessly; several times the tip of his blade scored her flesh, and Aton saw her flinch and gasp. Blood-red scratches appeared on her skin.

She was hanging with her back to the post, facing out toward the crowd. Once again she and Aton looked at one another. She forced a weak smile, as if to tell him not to be alarmed by what he saw. Yet he could tell that she herself was afraid.

She closed her eyes, then, as the Initiator stepped forward and ran his hand over her body. He grunted with satisfaction, turned, and picked up a heavy bull-whip. Its braided leather was inset with a series of metal studs that gleamed in the sunlight.

The Initiator uncoiled the whip, and there was an expectant murmur in the crowd. He gestured to the guards to stand back, then turned to the King.

The King nodded. "Begin," he murmured.

The Initiator flexed his shoulders. He took a firm grip with both hands on the handle of the whip, swung it back in a wide arc, and brought it around with a savage crack.

Malice's scream was the cry of someone experiencing pleasure raised to a level that was unbearable. It roused sexual blood-lust in the men in the crowd—

and in the women, too, so far as Aton could see. All of them pressed forward, staring avidly at Malice's naked flesh, defaced now with a bright pink welt and red dots of blood.

Aton found he was sweating profusely. He felt himself trembling. The Minion half of his personality was responding horribly to the vision in front of him. He not only savored her pain, but craved more. Worse, he found himself imagining how it might feel if he was the one up there, beating the beautiful woman dangling from her wrists. The idea was intolerable; yet it possessed him.

The Initiator swung the whip again, and again. Malice cried out from deep in her throat, and it sounded as though she were dying of ecstasy.

Aton looked away, but hearing the torture without seeing it was even worse. He put his hands over his ears, but he could still hear the braided leather striking Malice's flesh, and there was no way to shut out her screams.

He paced to and fro, tension building inside him. Finally he found himself moving around the crowd to the side of the platform. He started taking longer, faster strides.

No one noticed him, at first; all eyes were on the spectacle. He reached the right-hand edge of the platform. It was only three feet above the ground. He leaped onto it.

He caught a brief glimpse of the crowd, faces turning toward him, staring up, stupid with surprise. The King grabbed the sides of his chair and shouted something, and one of the guards moved forward, drawing his sword.

Aton faced the guard moving toward him. He karate-kicked the man in the stomach, knocking him off his feet. The guard hit the platform with a crash, rolled over, and lay holding his head and moaning.

Two of the other guards reached for their weapons. Aton stooped and seized the sword of the man he had just felled. He raised it warningly.

The two guards glanced at one another, then ran toward him with their blades drawn. Aton's mouth was dry and his head was buzzing. He leaped outside the first man's thrust and swung his own blade around, slicing it into the back of the man's neck. The other guard hesitated, and Aton slashed the tip of his sword across the man's face. He dropped his weapon, clutched his head in his hands, and screamed. Blood poured out from between his fingers.

People were shouting. Aton turned quickly as the three remaining guards released the two women they had been holding and drew their swords. Aton took a step toward them—but thick braided leather suddenly held him back, coiling around his throat, studs jabbing his skin. The Initiator had swung his whip, and now he jerked it, trying to pull Aton off his feet.

Aton yelled with fury. He turned and hacked the leather with his sword, but it flexed and absorbed the blow.

He charged toward the hooded man holding the handle of the whip. The Initiator backed away and jerked the whip again, but Aton was already on top of him. Aton drove the point of his sword squarely into the man's throat.

Somewhere above the screams of panic and shouts of pain he heard Malice calling to him, begging him to stop. But the remaining three guards were advancing on him, and his rage, now, was surging high. He pulled the whip from around his neck and threw it aside. He feinted left, then lashed out suddenly to the right and slashed one man's wrist, knocking the sword out of his hand. The second one charged forward, eyes wide with fear and desperation, but Aton crouched and swung his blade into his shin, sending him falling on his face.

The last guard hesitated. His eyes were wide, his face was pale, confronted with this raging giant. Aton picked up a sword that one of his other adversaries had dropped, and hurled it at the guard in front of him. It skewered him in the chest, and he fell, crying out in horror.

Aton turned toward the crowd in the square. They were backing away, trampling one another, terrified. He swayed on his feet and shook sweat out of his eyes, all his muscles trembling. He glanced left and right, as if expecting to find more of the King's men pouring into the square. But no one appeared. He was standing alone on the platform under the bright sun.

He strode to the wooden post and slashed the rope. Malice dropped down onto her feet, naked and bleeding. "Aton," she sobbed, "please, you mustn't—"

He grabbed her wrists, still tied together with the remainder of the rope, and dragged her with him to the side of the stage. The King was there in his chair, too obese to haul himself out of it. His Minionette slaves backed away whimpering in fear, their chains jingling.

Aton raised his sword. The tip of it wavered erratically. "Safe passage," he told the King. He took a deep breath, trying to steady himself. "You'll give me safe passage out of here. And her." He gestured to Malice. "Tell your men—"

His voice died as he saw the small black shape that the King was holding. It was a modern nerve gun, usable only at close range, but highly effective.

The beam bathed Aton and his muscles went into spasms. The sword fell out of his hands. He collapsed onto the wooden planks, his limbs fluttering.

The villagers carried Aton to an empty hut and tied him and Malice to two wooden chairs. The hut had holes in its thatched roof and smelled wet and rancid. The glass in its window had long since been broken, and had been replaced with a square of stained sackcloth. When the villagers shut and locked the door, the interior was plunged into semidarkness.

While Aton slumped limp and semi-comatose in his chair, Malice sat in silence, staring at her hands in her lap. Noises from outside were muted and indistinct; there was no way to tell what was happening.

After half an hour Aton felt waves of tingling warmth spreading through him, and he began to regain most of his motor functions. He swallowed awkwardly and managed to turn his head. "Are you—

all right?" he asked her, speaking with difficulty, his voice sounding clumsy and strained.

"Of course." She raised her head and looked at him with mournful eyes. "And you?"

"The—stun charge is wearing off." He moved his arms experimentally, then his legs. The ropes tying him to the chair were not tight, but were quite sufficient to stop him from breaking free. "What—do you think they'll do?"

"You really want to know?"

He nodded.

She drew a shaky breath. "They'll torture you publicly, then execute you."

"But, Federation law—"

"Yes, by law a Proscribed planet should turn over an intruder to the nearest Federation outpost. But they won't do that. They despise offworlders."

"I see." He looked around at the grimy little hut, its floor of damp earth and its rafters of rotten wood. His own world of Hvee had been poor, but it hadn't had Minion's pervasive reek of deprivation and decay. So this was what he had gained as a result of all his striving to possess the woman now sitting beside him.

"I've been thinking while I've been sitting here," she said, "that in a way it's all my fault. When your father came to Minion twenty-five years ago, I was the one who broke the taboo against relations with an offworld man. I was too young, too rebellious to understand the possible consequences. I don't know if you can ever forgive me for that."

"For *being my mother*?" He laughed unpleasantly at

the way the words sounded. It was the first time he had actually been able to say them, since he'd found her and she had told him the truth, just two days before. He shook his head. "The only thing I can't forgive you the way you imprinted me, seduced my soul, when I was too young to understand or defend myself."

"But you were my son! I yearned to have you as my lover!"

"Only here, in this twisted culture, is that thinkable."

"It's *your* culture, Aton."

He turned and glared at her. A sliver of sunlight filtered around the cloth nailed over the window and touched the side of her neck and face. Her naked body was an indistinct pale shape, but he could easily see the wounds inflicted by the Initiator's whip. "I disown a culture that strips women naked and publicly beats them to death."

"Oh, Aton, you still don't understand." She stared at him with soft, sad eyes.

"I understand that you were afraid." His emotions were making it hard for him to speak. "When they tied you to that post, you were terrified."

"I was only afraid that the experience would be too intense. Sometimes, it can be fatal. But most of all I was full of grief because you wouldn't be the one who was beating me."

He moved restlessly in his bonds. "That's insane."

"No." She shook her head emphatically. "You felt the same way too. I saw it in your eyes. Deep down, you wanted it to be you, not the Initiator, wielding the whip."

"That's not so."

"Then why did you run wild and kill those men? You couldn't face your own desire to hurt me, so you hurt them instead. You were jealous of them, Aton, and it was the only outlet for your rage."

He closed his eyes, remembering, too well, his emotions. On Hvee, he had been trained in martial arts—but as a discipline, not as a technique for mass murder.

They were silent in the little room for a while. "I don't even understood the purpose of the Initiations," he said eventually. "None of it makes any sense."

"Any single woman has an obligation to marry and start a new family line. Minion is poor; it needs more people. A woman who remains single and childless for more than three years is initiated into the King's harem. He makes her pregnant, and she gives birth to a son, who matures, then becomes the father of her next son, and so on. The Initiations are just a ritual to prove that a woman is strong and fit enough."

"My God," he whispered, "you mean you would have ended up pregnant by that disgusting little—"

"It was not my choice!" she cried. "I thought you and I would be safe here. The Initiations are usually over by this time of the year. When the guards arrived at my cabin, how could I have stopped them from taking me? I was afraid if I revealed you to them, they would see you were not pure Minion. Your name wouldn't be in the census, they would turn you over to the Federation, or worse. I tried to protect you, don't you see?"

There was a long silence. "I'm sorry," he muttered.

"Aton, you should have used the disk I gave you,

and saved yourself. You should never have tried to rescue me. I wish you hadn't done what you did."

"All right, all right! But it almost worked. How was I to know the King would be armed with a modern weapon? Technology is supposed to be outlawed on a Proscribed planet."

"Don't you *care* that you killed two people?" Her voice was suddenly shrill. "You talk about our twisted morality—but you killed two innocent men, and wounded five more."

The door of the hut was thrown open before Atón had a chance to reply. He winced in the sudden sunlight. Three soldiers were silhouetted against the glare.

"There he is, Sergeant," one of them said.

"All right, let's take a look." A man bent down and squinted at Aton's face. His breath smelled of beer and tobacco, and he wore several days' growth of beard. "Yeah, offworlder, sure enough." He gestured at Malice. "She have relations with him?"

"No one knows anything about 'em, Sergeant."

"Well, we'll soon find out. Put 'em in the carts outside—separately. We'll take 'em back to the palace."

"Yes, sir."

"Watch yourself. He's from a high-grav planet by the look of him. Strong bastard."

"I demand to be returned to the Federation," Aton said. "You have no jurisdiction over me."

The sergeant laughed. "You *demand*, do you?"

"I am a Federation citizen. Under the law, no peasant planet—"

"Peasants, are we?" The man spat on the floor.

"Let me tell you something, mister. There's never been a war here. Not even any fighting to speak of. A man gets an urge to hit someone, he takes it home to his wife, where it belongs." He pointed a finger at Aton's face. "But a man who gets violent outside his family, him we make an example of. Just to make sure no one else gets the same idea."

"But Federation law—"

The sergeant raised his booted foot and kicked Aton in the chest. Aton's chair tipped over and fell on its back with a crash, taking him with it. "Screw your Federation. You come here, kill people, we deal with you our own way." He gestured to the guards. "Get this bastard over to the palace jail." He turned his back and walked away.

chapter v _____

Dream-memories of Minion dissolved into darkness. As Aton struggled to focus his eyes he saw the green-and-black mosaic of phosphorescent lichen on walls of stone, and knew he was back in the labyrinths of Chthon.

Something was tossing him bodily to and fro, and with each jolt pain flashed from the side of his skull. He tried to sit up, and found there was a leathery blanket restraining him. He twisted, squirmed, and discovered he was trapped in a sack made from rough animal hide, large enough to enclose him completely with only his head protruding. The mouth of the sack had been gathered tightly and tied with a leather thong around his neck.

Aton looked down and found that the sack was lashed to the back of a huge animal, plodding slowly along a wide tunnel. To one side of him was the animal's flank, sprouting coarse hairs from pale, scaly skin. Further up he was just able to glimpse the back of the beast's head, round and matted with fur. Each step it took jostled and swung him from side to side.

"Aton?"

He turned his head, and the sack chafed his skin where it was secured around his neck. He found Oris close by, bundled like himself, dangling on the other side of the animal's back.

"How long was I out?" he asked her.

"Maybe half an hour."

"It felt like days. I remembered—" He broke off, haunted by chromatic images of Minion that still lived inside his eyes. "Are you injured?"

"No." She paused as if it would cost her something to tell him more. "I hit my head. I was dazed for a while."

"What happened to the thing that attacked us?"

"We're on it."

Again, Aton tried to see the animal. It walked on all fours, yet most of its weight seemed to be on its hind legs, and a tail dragged behind it. He remembered glimpsing its giant incisors when it had attacked him. "Yet it didn't kill us," he said.

Oris didn't answer.

The tunnel was growing wider, and the lichen-glow was brighter ahead. Within another minute the creature emerged into a huge chamber whose roof receded hundreds of feet above.

The animal lurched to a halt. Aton felt immense muscles moving under its hide, and then it vented a deep barking noise that vibrated through him.

There was an answering bellow from ahead. The beast moved forward and passed through a gap in a mounded wall of boulders. On top of the wall, twenty or thirty feet above, Aton glimpsed two more of the huge beasts. They looked like a cross between apes and lizards. Their baleful simian eyes watched him pass below, through the entrance into their kingdom.

"But this is the place," Aton exclaimed. "This is what I was searching for, the sanctuary I remembered." The contours were so familiar—yet so wrong. Here, he was sure, he had cultivated a garden of Hvee flowers. There had been a waterfall, a gently sloping meadow of soft grass, a stream full of exotic fish.

Yet from his vantage point on the back of the creature he saw an arid, hostile place, hazy with dust, inhabited by monsters.

Half a dozen of the animals were toiling in a shallow pit, digging with clawed front feet. The rock seemed soft, like sandstone, and it powdered easily. Aton saw one of them stoop, pluck a black object from the ground, and throw it onto a heap of oily nuggets.

Further on, dark water flowed sluggishly from a fissure in the side of the cavern and formed a wide, stagnant pool where several more of the animals were wading to and fro. The pool had been formed by damming the river with a wall of rocks, stacked loosely so that meager trickles of water escaped between them. Aton realized that the dam was a primitive filter—a net that would allow small fish to pass through while trapping larger ones. He saw one of the wading animals slash its paw down suddenly into the pool, then straighten up, clutching a pale, flopping thing that it dashed into lifelessness on a nearby boulder.

He and Oris were carried past the dam along a

path beside the continuation of the river. The water had carved a meandering channel down the center of the cave, and the sandstone either side had been eroded into flat areas of sodden mud. Here, large plants had taken root: strange knobbly vines and root things, ghostly pale and devoid of leaves. They were giant fungi, surviving in the absence of sunlight on nothing more than air, water, and trace minerals in the soil. Two huge furry-headed figures were plucking appendages from the vines and stuffing them in sacks that dangled from their shoulders. They paused and watched dully as Oris and Aton were carried past.

Ahead, Aton saw that the river disappeared into a narrow slit in the end wall of the cave. Close by was a mosaic of holes in the rock—windows of an elaborate dwelling that had been quarried out of the sandstone. A long flight of stone stairs ascended to a big archway that seemed to be its entrance. The animal carrying him and Oris started plodding up the steps.

"You ever hear of anything like this?" Aton asked her.

She didn't answer.

"Look, neither of us likes the situation. But if we don't cooperate, at this point, we don't have a chance."

She eyed him coldly. "What makes you think we have a chance if we do?"

"They could have killed us if they'd wanted to. We've breen brought back here for a reason."

She thought about that. "Maybe so. But I don't see any way out."

The creature carried them through the archway,

into a murky hand-hewn chamber. Here, finally, the ape-reptile set them down on the ground. Aton flinched as the beast's long claws fumbled with the thong binding his sack and loosened it, so it fell open around his shoulders. He wriggled free, shaky but uninjured except for the bruise on the side of his head, which still throbbed painfully.

Aton watched as the creature released Oris. Now that he was further from it, he saw its real size. Squatting on its hind legs, it was twelve feet tall. Its hide had the shiny wrinkles of snakeskin, overlaid with thin black hairs. Its short pointed tail was grayish pink. Hair grew more densely on its head, which was bulbous, with a crescent-shaped mouth and close-spaced eyes. It looked almost like a gigantic human fetus, covered with a sprinkling of fur.

Aton retreated from it till his back was against the wall. He looked around warily at the rest of the chamber.

Green lichen-glow filtered in through two big windows that looked out onto the rest of the cavern. The floor was dark with dirt, and littered with bones. In its center was a tier of steps that led up to a dais where there was a stone throne. Beside that stood an ornately carved urn where something was smoldering dully, making the chamber hazy with fumes.

Seated in the throne, looking down impassively on Aton, was an emaciated old man. He was totally naked, though much of his withered torso was concealed by a white beard that lay like matted cobwebs across his chest. His head, too, was festooned with white hair, so that the only visible features of his face were his eyes, glinting in the gloom. Where his pallid skin was revealed, it was mottled with dark, festering sores.

Aton took a tentative step forward.

"Stop there, you." The old man's voice was high-pitched and the words had a strange lilt to them. He gestured, and Aton heard a deep, warning growl from his left. The ape-lizard was watching Aton intently, squatting on its haunches, its clawed front feet dangling within easy reach of him.

The old man stood up. "My babies take care of me," he said. He chuckled as he started down the steps from his dais. "They protect me, they provide for me. Bless 'em, they wouldn't know what to do without me."

"So you're the architect," said Aton. "Everything in here and out there"—he gestured through one of the windows at the rest of the huge cavern—"is your work."

The old man paused on the last step. "My babies performed the labor. I just gave them the plan." His old eyes blinked in the dimness and he looked from Aton to Oris, and back again. "So. On the hard trek, eh? Is that it?"

"Yes," said Oris.

The old man shook his head, and his white hair swirled around him. "Stupid waste of time. There's no way out."

"How can you be so sure?" Oris's voice was strong, but Aton sensed fear in it. Without her group of followers she seemed smaller, now, and less of a commanding presence.

The old man pointed at her. "You don't answer back to me, woman. You show some respect. I know ten times more than you'll ever know."

Oris glanced uneasily at the huge beast still squatting at one side of the chamber. She said nothing.

"Where's the rest of your people?" the old man demanded.

Oris shook her head. "I—don't understand."

He made a complicated sign-gesture. The creature reached out quickly. Talons wrapped themselves around Oris's body, trapping her arms by her sides and flattening her breasts. The creature lifted her off the floor and tightened its grip, crushing her. She screamed and thrashed her legs helplessly.

Aton started forward, then stopped as he saw the beast's other arm poised and ready for him.

The old man gave a high-pitched laugh. "My babies understand. Oh yes." He made another gesture and the beast released some of its pressure on Oris, though still holding her six feet above the floor. "Woman, don't lie to me. It takes more than two to make the trek. Think I don't know that? Eh? So where's the rest of you?"

"We're the last survivors," Oris gasped, prying futilely at the claws clutching her.

The old man scowled. "You trash, I'll—"

"There are sixteen others in our group," Aton cut in. "But we two were on our own, when your—animal—found us."

The old man chewed on his beard. "Hm, hm. Go on."

"When I last saw the others, they were cutting up the body of a glowmole. I don't know exactly where that was."

The old man grunted. "Well. All right." He waved his arm and the creature released Oris, letting her fall to the floor. She lay there for a moment, clutching her bruised ribs and gasping for breath. She shot Aton a confused, angry look.

Aton ignored her. "You must be short of food," he said to the old man.

"Eh? What's that?"

"We wondered why there was no wildlife. Your creatures must have hunted it to extinction around here. But once in a while I suppose you come across convicts making the hard trek. You bring them in, play with them for a while, then kill them and eat them, is that it?"

The old man blinked at Aton. He seemed to be searching for words.

"Meanwhile your population out there keeps growing. Your—babies—don't understand birth control, do they?" Aton shook his head. "You'll be eating each other, before long."

"That's enough." The old man made a threatening gesture, and the animal beside him growled and shuffled forward. "I won't listen to this—"

"You should get out while you can," Aton interrupted. "Join us, find a way out of Chthon, and stop living like a cannibal."

"Enough!" he shouted. He pointed to Aton, then Oris, then to the corner of the chamber. "You'll go downstairs and join your friends."

The creature groped in the dirt in the corner and pulled a tapered stone plug out of a hole in the floor. It seized Oris around the waist and dropped her down the hole. Aton ran for the door, but the beast grabbed him by the neck, dragged him back, and thrust him, too, into darkness.

chapter vi _____

There were two men in the darkness whose voices Aton could identify: Jacko, and Votnik. There were three more: the man named Snyder, another whose name was Rogers, and a woman who said her name was Gwinnie.

"Ape-thing came in at us from one end of the tunnel," Snyder was saying, "while we were cutting up the glowmole. Its body blocked the way out, so wasn't nothing we could do. It picked us off one at a time."

"I slashed it." Jacko's voice: "Slashed it in the face."

"That didn't stop it. Didn't even slow it down," said Snyder.

"Still, I slashed it."

"It took your knife away," Snyder persisted.

"I put up a fight. That's more than anyone else did."

"Quiet!" Oris's voice was a sudden slap of sound.

There was silence. The cell was totally black, and the stench of flesh was overpowering. By feeling his way with outstretched fingers Aton had determined it was about ten feet in diameter, seven or eight feet high, with a stone ceiling, stone walls, and a floor of volcanic rock. In the center of the floor was a six-inch lava tube that served as a toilet. In one of the walls was a huge stone plug, like the one in the ceiling that had been briefly removed to allow himself and Oris into this prison. The only other feature he'd been able to find was a small hole in one wall, admitting a trickle of air. It was the sole source of ventilation.

"What about the others, back where we sat down to eat?" Oris asked. "What happened to them?"

"No way of knowing," said Jacko. "My guess is, maybe they came looking for us when we didn't show up, they saw there'd been a fight and we was gone, so they got the hell out of there, if they had any sense."

"No way they could come and rescue us from this, anyhow," said Snyder.

There was another silence.

"I don't know how much longer I can stand it in here," said Rogers. "Oris, you got to realize, we been down here a couple hours longer than you." He made a gasping noise, as if he were having trouble breathing. "You got to realize—"

"All right, all right, my friend," said Votnik. "We know how you feel."

"They wouldn't have bothered to lock us in here," Aton pointed out, "unless they planned to let us out eventually."

"That don't make sense," said Jacko.

"It does. If you have no use for a man, you kill

him. But if you want him for some future purpose, you keep him prisoner."

"Well, I'll allow as there's some truth to that," said Votnik. "But do you have any clue, my friend, what that future purpose might be?"

"Of course he doesn't." Oris sounded scornful, but unsure of herself beneath the bravado.

"Well, the old man didn't disagree with me when I suggested he was short of food," Aton said.

"Let me make sure I understand you," Votnik said. "You're referring to the old man in the chamber above us, with the white hair?"

"The zoo keeper," Aton said grimly. "Keeper of the apetiles."

"Apetiles, yes. That's what they are. And he agreed with you when you said—"

"Those animals are enormous; they must have a huge food intake. Judging from their teeth, they're carnivores. Since the old man obviously cares more about them than about us—calls them his 'babies'—I'm sure he plans to use us as food."

"Oh Jesus." Rogers's voice rose to a whine. "I don't know how much longer—"

"Gwinnie, hold him," snapped Oris.

"Where are you?" Gwinnie's voice came from right beside Aton in the blackness. He felt her blundering around, searching for Rogers, who had started sobbing quietly to himself.

"Oris, do you think Aton's right?" said Snyder.

"I think he's full of shit."

"Only because you didn't work it out for yourself," Aton told her.

"Want me to shut him up, Oris?" Jacko asked. "Me, I already had more than enough of—"

"Easy, easy," Votnik interrupted. "This is no time to fight among ourselves. I'm sure none of us questions Oris's authority here. None of us, *including you*, Aton. Wouldn't you say so, my friend?"

Aton smiled to himself in the darkness. "Of course."

"Well, then. Live and let live."

"But if they're going to use us for food," Snyder whined, "how come they didn't kill us already?"

"That I don't know," said Aton.

"Where'd those apetiles come from, anyway?" said Gwinnie. "We never seen nothing as weird as them before."

"Mutations," Aton told her. "Generations ago, they were human. Maybe there are radioactive ores in the rock. You noticed that the old man had skin cancers? Also, I think we're significantly closer to the center of Chthon; the gravity—"

"Mister, your gabbing gives me headache," growled Jacko. "Quit it, all right?"

Aton had a clear mental image of each person's position in the prison. Using the martial arts training of his childhood, he had assembled all the tiny cues—the characteristic sounds of breathing, movement, and speech. He could visualize Jacko; or Oris, for that matter. He could kill either of them in the total darkness, and there would be no way for anyone to know who had done it.

But Oris could be valuable to him; and as for Jacko, it wasn't yet time. "I didn't mean to get on anyone's nerves," he said blandly.

"Bullshit!"

"Oris," Rogers interrupted plaintively, "should we pray to Chthon?"

There was a long pause. "Not now, Rogers." She sounded weary.

"Friends, if you don't mind my saying so, I think we should rest to conserve our strength," said Votnik.

"Right," said Oris. "Votnik is right."

Crammed together in the small space, the seven of them stretched out as well as they could. Aton chose a spot as near as possible to the fresh-air inlet, and leaned with his back to the wall. He stayed alert in case Jacko might decide to come looking for him, but the big man seemed to settle down on the opposite side of the cell, near where Gwinnie was still trying to comfort Rogers.

Several hours had passed since Aton last ate, and he felt the cold gnawing at him from inside as well as out. His reserves of strength were almost exhausted; and yet, strangely, he felt no fear. Somehow, he sensed, he would survive.

An hour dragged by, but he did not sleep. His mind wandered through memories, checking and probing. There had been another woman, after the Minionette had died (yes; he was sure she had died; though he still didn't know if he had killed her). A woman named Coquina, who'd shared his life in Chthon, and borne a son, Arlo. He'd loved her—hadn't he?—although never with the same intensity he'd felt for Malice. Had that been while he was a prisoner in the garnet mines? Each new fact prompted ten new questions, and there were still so few answers. . . .

There was a grinding noise, and the floor shuddered. A ring of dim light became visible. Aton hauled himself up onto his feet. Someone or something was outside, removing the stone plug from the hole in the wall. As it was withdrawn, green radiance flooded in.

Aton was the first to emerge. He found himself out in the cavern, on a big square of rocky ground bordered by huge slabs of shale that formed walls ten feet high. Four of the apetiles were crouched in this arena, like mutant cats around a mouse hole. They watched in silence as the human prisoners stumbled out. Rogers was the last to emerge, and when he saw the creatures he tried to retreat. But one of them held him while another jammed the stone plug back in its hole.

"Please, not to be alarmed." The voice came from above. Aton looked up and saw the old man standing in one of the windows of his home. Beside him was the stone urn that had rested near his throne, cupping a dim, smoky flame. Coal, Aton realized; that was the black stuff he had seen the apetiles clawing out of the shallow pit near the entrance to the cavern. Fire must have some mystical significance to the creatures; the old man used it as a symbol of his power over them.

"These four boys"—the old man gestured to the gigantic figures towering over them—"are my best hunters. But even the best need practice, to keep fit."

He gave his high-pitched chuckle. "Which is why you're here."

"Gladiatorial games," said Votnik. His face had turned pale and the plump skin was sagging.

Aton shook his head. "You're thinking in human terms. We're not human, to him. We're insects that he's going to feed to his pets."

"Now, I don't expect you to fight all of them at once," the old man went on. He made a cryptic gesture, and three of the four apetiles clambered out over the ten-foot walls. "And each of you will have a weapon." He tossed some glittering objects down into the arena. They were crudely forged daggers, less than five inches long. "If any of you survives, you'll go free. Really, I wish you the best of luck."

"There'll be no survivors," Aton said grimly.

Oris turned on him. "You don't know that."

"I do." Aton made no move to pick up one of the daggers. "He has no reason to let anyone live."

"Well, I ain't going out without a fight," said Jacko. He bent down and grabbed the largest of the knives.

"Then you're a fool," said Aton.

"You got a better way to save your neck?"

"Get ready, there," the old man called to them, peering down from his vantage point.

"That thing isn't the enemy," said Aton, gesturing at the apetile crouching at the opposite end of the arena. "He is." He jerked his head toward the old man in the window above.

Jacko eyed the sheer wall. "No way to—"

"One well-aimed rock," said Aton. "With him dead,

and no one else to give them orders, his creatures won't know what to do."

Jacko licked his lips. He shifted his grip on the dagger. "All right, so you throw the rock."

Aton shook his head. "I'm not strong enough, and my aim isn't good enough."

"Begin!" the old man shouted from above.

The apetile snarled and started forward.

Rogers panicked. He screamed, ran blindly for one of the shale walls, collided with it, and started scrabbling at the smooth rock. He shat and pissed in fear as the apetile turned and lumbered toward him. It picked him up in one huge paw, and bit his head off. There was the crunching of jaws on bone. Blood gushed in a huge fountain.

Oris moaned and clutched herself. Aton turned on Jacko. "Do it, man!"

"All right, all right!" He threw down his dagger, ran to the center of the arena, and grabbed a large, round stone.

The apetile tossed aside Rogers's corpse and licked blood off its paw.

Jacko drew back his arm. His face contorted with a mixture of fear and rage. He hurled the stone.

It struck the old man in the center of his forehead. He gave a fractured cry, tottered to one side, and groped for the edge of the window where he stood. His fingers missed their hold. He waved his arms wildly but lost his balance and fell, plummeting head-first into the arena below. There was an ugly snapping noise as he hit the ground, and he lay still.

The apetile in the yard, and the three outside it,

stood and stared. Finally, one of the ones outside uttered a deafening guttural scream. It scrambled in over the wall, with the other two following behind, converging on Jacko.

"Come on!" Aton yelled. He shoved Votnik toward the nearest wall and gestured for Oris, Snyder, and Gwinnie to follow. "Don't look!" he shouted, as Gwinnie turned and saw the apetiles ripping Jacko apart in an orgy of revenge.

"I'll never make it," Votnik stammered, staring up, his face quivering.

"Help me," Aton snapped at Oris, grabbing the fat man from one side.

She hesitated only for a moment. Together, they pushed him over the top. Aton went up next, reached back, and hauled Gwinnie after him. She helped Snyder up, and then Oris.

They leaped down the other side. "What now?" said Votnik. "Out the way we came in?"

"No." Several of the creatures near the main entrance of the cave had turned their heads, puzzled by the noises from the arena. "It has to be the river." He ran toward the gully where the water disappeared into a narrow slit in the rockface.

"It'll kill us!" Snyder protested.

"No other way," Aton insisted. "Take deep breaths. Don't jump till you have to. Load your blood with oxygen." He glanced back and saw one of the apetiles in the arena raise its head and peer over the wall. Its mouth was smeared with Jacko's blood, and fragments of his skin clung to its teeth. It gave an angry cry, clambered up and over the wall, and started toward them.

"Now," said Aton. He leaped into the river.

The others splashed in after him. The water was frighteningly cold, like a wedge of ice driven into his abdomen. He kept his head above the surface, still gulping air.

The dark slit in the rockface came nearer, and he heard the water gurgling into it. It was six or eight feet wide, but barely a foot high. Aton leaned back in the water and let the current suck his legs into the crevice. He slid in, and the edges scraped his belly and his back. Votnik bumped up behind him and he grabbed the man's feet, hauling him after him.

The water closed over Aton's head. He felt himself plummeting, turning, the water gripping him, sucking him down. He tried to swim, but the current was too powerful. He reached out, but his hands found only more water. It pressed in on his face and body, holding him, claiming him.

CHAPTER 5 _____

They handcuffed Aton, secured his ankles with a length of chain, and tied him in the back of a horse-drawn cart. Two soldiers sat either side of him, and the sergeant took the driver's seat. When Aton attempted to talk to them, they refused to reply.

The cart bumped along at little more than walking pace. The sun was still high and Aton sweated through the journey, watching the Minion countryside roll slowly by while a second cart, carrying Malice, followed behind.

Finally they reached a village that seemed slightly larger than the one where he had witnessed the Initiations. Word had obviously spread ahead of him: Minion men and their wives stood in the doorways of their hovels and glared at him as he was carried past. Some shouted abuse; a few children threw stones.

At the top of a hill overlooking the village, the King's palace turned out to be a ramshackle two-story building made of logs. A pair of sentries armed with pikes and spears opened a gate in a stone wall, and the carts moved along a gravel track that took them to the back of the building. The sergeant jumped down and tethered the horse while his men lifted Aton off the cart, his chains making it impossible for him to step down unaided.

A gleaming shape caught his attention, half hidden behind trees bordering the palace grounds. At first he feared it was Malice's transit capsule, called down from orbit somehow by the King's men. But that was impossible; the disk in his pocket provided the only link. As he looked more carefully he realized that this silver vehicle was larger, and of a different design. A few times in his years roaming through space he had seen ships like it, operated by Xests, spidery creatures who constituted one of three intelligent alien species in the known galaxy. They usually preferred to interact with humans as little as possible.

He had no time to wonder what a Xest ship was doing here on a Proscribed world. The guards hustled him into the palace. He caught one last glimpse of Malice being taken to a different entrance, and then a thick wooden door slammed behind him.

They led him down to the basement and put him behind iron bars in a small cell with straw on the floor. It smelled like a stable and, in fact, horses were kept nearby—he heard one of them whinny, and smelled their droppings. The only light came from a high, barred window, and Aton was left alone for several hours, watching the sky fade from blue to purple to black. The place seemed seldom used; there was only one other cell, and it was empty.

Finally the sergeant returned with a dozen guards behind him, some carrying swords, a couple others lighting the way with oil lamps. The sergeant himself was holding a nerve gun that looked like the one the King had used in the village square. Quite possibly, it was the only weapon of its kind on the planet.

He made Aton back away from the cell door, then opened it, entered, and locked it again behind him, while the guards stood outside.

"All right, you bastard." The sergeant's breath smelled more strongly of beer than before, and his cheeks glowed red. He belched behind his hand and gestured for Aton to sit on the one item of furniture in the cell, a battered three-legged milking stool. "I been told to tell you what's been decided. You'll be disemboweled, then stoned to death, in the village square at noon tomorrow." He paused to blow his nose into his hand, then wiped his fingers on his breeches.

"Maybe you remember the Initiator," he went on. "The one you stabbed in the throat. Killed him, as it happened. Well, his son's going to be the one cutting you up tomorrow. Seems to me, if I was him, I'd probably do my best to make the job last awhile.

"But you got a choice," he concluded. "You cooperate with us, tell us some things we'd like to know, and I'll see they slip you some herbs beforehand that'll kill the pain. Understand what I'm saying?"

Aton shook his head. "I don't make bargains with peasants."

The sergeant stared at him for a minute. "All right, so I'll make sure and give 'em a blunt knife to use on you, you bastard." He belched again and swayed slightly. "It don't matter whether you talk or not, anyhow. Your woman already confessed. I think she thought we'd go easy on you if we knew you got half-Minion blood." He laughed scornfully. "The way I see it, there's only one thing lower than an offworlder, and that's a half-breed."

"Where is she?" Aton stood up. He imagined her lying in the King's bedroom, with the grotesque little fat man between her thighs, panting over her perfect body. He took a shuffling step toward the sergeant, dragging his chains. "What's happening to her?"

"Wouldn't you like to know, eh?" The sergeant coughed and spat. "You won't be seeing her again. All right, there's one thing you got, the way I understand it, that the King wants. Looks like a coin, except it ain't. Talk into it, and a spaceship comes down from the sky." He paused. "I hope you wasn't thinking of using it, 'cause I'm going to take it off you."

Aton sat back down on the stool. So long as he'd had the disk, he'd felt there was some hope of escape.

"There's two ways we can manage this," said the sergeant." You hand it over, or—" He raised the nerve gun. "I never used one of these gadgets before, but I'd be happy to try."

Aton realized he should have hidden the disk; but even if he'd done so, they would have found it by searching his cell. He didn't like to think what they might have done to Malice to get her to confess that it was in his possession.

"I'm going to count one, two, three," the sergeant was saying. "And if I get to three—"

Aton fumbled in his pocket. "Here," he said.

The sergeant kept the gun ready in one hand while

he reached out with the other. He moved cautiously, as if he expected Aton to throw his chains off somehow and attack. He snatched the disk out of Aton's fingers and moved back to the door of the cell. "All right," he said. "Now we got what we want." He took out his bunch of keys, opened the cell door, stepped out, and locked it again behind him.

Aton went to the bars. "I don't care what you do to me. I just want to know about Malice."

The sergeant ignored him. He turned to his men. "I'll stand first watch. Leave one of those lamps down here so's I can see to eat my supper. You, Sadler, take this thing up to the King. He wants it right away." He handed the disk to one of the men, who walked out staring at it as if it might be dangerous.

"You, Mason," the sergeant went on, "relieve me at midnight. The rest of you, be here eight o'clock sharp to take out the prisoner." He paused and grinned. "King told me he wants a rope tied to this bastard's balls so's they can drag him through the village behind a donkey. That'll give people a chance to throw some cow shit at him before his guts get cut out at midday." He sniggered.

There was laughter among the guards as they walked out, their booted footsteps echoing on the stone floor.

Aton sat on the stool and leaned against the wall, his hands manacled in front of him. He stared blankly ahead, through the bars of his cell, at the empty cell opposite.

The sergeant made himself comfortable on a chair beside the door at the far end of the basement. After a while Aton heard someone arrive with food, and there was the sound of a metal dish being set down. Aton smelled roast chicken, and heard the sergeant start tearing into it, pausing occasionally to gulp beer from a jug.

Evidently they didn't observe the custom of giving a condemned man one last meal.

Time dragged by. Aton was still sitting in the same position, three hours later, when he saw the Xest.

At first he thought he was hallucinating. It looked as if the mounds of straw were shifting by themselves on the floor of the other prison cell. Then, suddenly, he understood: the Xest's yellow body and eight spidery legs blended in so well that he had failed to distinguish it from its surroundings.

Aton walked to the bars. Xests were passive telepaths: they could receive another entity's thoughts, but could not transmit. They were mute, so that the only way they could talk to human beings, without electronic assistance, was by sign language.

Having served in space for four years, Aton had picked up the galactic signing vocabulary. He peered through the bars into the cell opposite, in the dim flickering light from the sergeant's oil lamp, and watched the Xest as it attempted to communicate.

CHAPTER 6 _____

"Human Self is alone." The alien's legs twitched, signing the cryptic statement.

Yes, Aton thought.

"Yet Human Self is two persons."

Aton paused, wondering what the alien meant. It was well known that Xests were confused by the concept of two human sexes. They had only one gender themselves, and reproduced by fission.

Then Aton understood. *You mean I am a half-breed*, he thought. *You heard the sergeant say so.*

"A half-breed, yes." The Xest paused as if thinking deeply. "One finds this of great philosophical interest."

I'm sorry, I don't feel like discussing that right now.

"What better way to spend the night before your dissolution than in philosophical discourse?"

I'd prefer to find a way out of here.

"Xest Self has been contemplating that problem for several days. No solution seems possible."

Why are you here? Why are they keeping you prisoner?

"Xest Self arrives as an ambassador, a sociobiologist also, studying the human species. Xest Self journeys from world to world. Has special diplomatic privilege to visit this Proscribed planet and study human genetics. Left all technological aids in ship, deferring to undeveloped status of this world. Nevertheless, arrested upon landing here and detained, papers confiscated. Xest Self has no recourse and is resigned to dissolution."

You mean they're going to kill you?

"In due course, yes, for trespass. At first they do attempt to communicate; but they are ignorant of universal sign language."

Aton stared at the alien. He remembered a video briefing he had once seen, depicting the Xest mode of reproduction. If any part of the alien was severed from its body, the cells reproduced, in an hour or less, creating an entirely new baby Xest complete in every detail. *But there is a way we can get out*, he thought, *if you're willing to sacrifice the tip of one of your legs.*

The Xest froze. Then, moving stiffly, it formed signs representing shock and revulsion.

The severed portion of yourself would regenerate. Isn't that right? It would be small enough to walk between the prison bars. The sergeant is already drunk; he'll soon pass out. Your smaller self can steal his keys.

"No, no!" the alien signed agitatedly. "You do not understand the debt!"

The debt? *Explain it to me.*

"Xest are many; resources are few. To reproduce oneself is to incur great debt to society. It is a debt one finds onerous to pay."

You'd rather let them kill you?

"Dissolution of the self is an honorable alternative for Xest species members, for it is the end to all debt."

For a human being, it's the worst fate imaginable.

The Xest made the sign that indicated regret coupled with unwillingness to lend assistance.

Aton paused for a moment, thinking carefully. *But what exactly do you mean by "dissolution"?*

"Ingestion of the body, so that regrowth becomes impossible. The Xest Self is assimilated by another. It is eaten."

But you're wrong! On Minion, if they want to kill you, they'll start by hacking you up with their swords.

The Xest remained immobile with shock for a full minute, absorbing the image in Aton's imagination. Aton embellished it with plausible detail: the Xest displayed on a platform in the village square in front of an expectant crowd. One of the King's guardsmen raising his sword. The Xest severed into ten or twenty pieces. And then, each piece regenerating—ten or twenty new Xests, scuttling around. More guardsmen drawing their swords, slicing and chopping. A hundred new Xests. A thousand.

"Stop!" the alien signed frantically. "It cannot be so!"

It is. They don't understand how you reproduce.

"You must tell them! The debt, the terrible debt—"

They wouldn't believe me. You heard how they talked to me. They think I'm lower than vermin.

Again the Xest lapsed immobile. Aton waited patiently. From the end of the basement, he heard the sergeant belch and shift position, making his chair creak. The man's breathing sounded heavy and regular.

It's a choice between a small debt, or a big one, Aton pointed out.

"Yes. Yes, one understands. There is no other way?"

None that I can think of.

"Very well."

Aton watched. The Xest moved toward the bars of its cell and wedged the end of one of its legs in the crack between the door and the metal frame. The alien paused, then shifted in a sudden spasm. There was a snapping sound. A four-inch segment of its leg fell to the floor.

"It is done."

How long does it take to grow?

"Soon, soon," the Xest signed lethargically, overwhelmed with remorse at having reproduced itself.

Minutes passed. There was a faint, tiny movement. The tip of the Xest's leg was changing visibly.

Can you communicate with your new self?

"We are both present, yes. Consciousness is shared among all cells. Growth is occurring. Patience." It paused. "When we are free," it signed hopefully, "Xest Self and Human Self can discuss human sexuality and genetics?"

Definitely. For as long as you want.

"That is some consolation."

The severed tip of the Xest's leg now had legs of its own. It looked like an unusually large, rather lumpy yellow caterpillar.

Aton heard the sergeant begin snoring. He didn't

know how much time was left before midnight, when the second shift would take over. *The keys!* he thought. *Get the keys!*

The mini-Xest crawled tentatively through the cell bars. It seemed to falter, then regained its balance. "One is newborn," the parent signaled to Aton. "One walks uncertainly."

Of course. I understand. He stood at the bars of his cell, watching as the offshoot of the alien tottered toward the end of the basement. Aton could see the sergeant's boots, stretched out beside a large beer jug lying on its side, but the rest of the man was hidden from his vantage point.

Finally, the mini-Xest reached the sleeping man.

Move gently, Aton thought. *Don't wake him!*

The little yellow crawling thing reached up with two tentative legs, and pulled itself onto the sergeant's breeches. Aton watched it move laboriously upward.

The keys were in his left pocket.

"Yes. They are still there."

There was a long moment of silence.

"The smaller self is too weak," the Xest signaled. "The man is lying on his side, on the pocket with the keys. The smaller self cannot extract them."

Aton groaned. *All right, climb higher and tickle his neck. Maybe he'll roll over.*

"The small self climbs."

Another minute passed. The sergeant stirred suddenly. He grunted and Aton heard him scratching. He yawned, muttered, and then settled again.

There was the sound of a bunch of keys falling onto the stone floor.

"The plan is successful," the Xest signed eagerly.

So far. Can your small self drag the keys down here?

"Yes. Small Xest is sufficiently strong and has great determination."

Faintly, Aton heard the keys scraping over the flagstones, through the straw. He clenched his hands around the bars of his cell, peering out impatiently. At last the little yellow shape came into view, one leg hooked around the big key ring, the other seven legs scrabbling diligently.

Aton squatted and reached out with both hands. He seized the keys and quickly found one that worked the lock of his manacles. He freed his ankles next, then started trying keys in the door of his cell one by one. The fourth attempt was successful; the door swung open.

He sidestepped around the little Xest and started toward the sergeant.

"Wait! Large Xest Self is not yet free!"

In a moment. Aton reached the sleeping man. He saw the nerve gun tucked inside the sergeant's tunic.

He positioned himself carefully, reached out till his fingers almost touched the man's chest, then pushed his hand down and grabbed the gun. The sergeant stirred, and his eyes flicked open. He saw Aton and his mouth fell wide in surprise.

"Quiet," Aton told him, leveling the gun at the man's face. "This thing can kill, if you know how to use it." That was a lie, but the sergeant wouldn't know any better.

The man nodded. He swallowed hard and tried to sit up in his chair. He licked his lips. "What do you—"

"I want Malice. The Minionette. Where is she?"

The sergeant shook his head. "She went. She's gone."

Aton pushed the gun closer to the man's face. "Where?"

"Offplanet. That's why they wanted the disk. To call her ship. They put her in it, sent it off."

Aton swore under his breath. "You're lying."

"No!" The man kept glancing at the nerve gun. He was obviously terrified. "Swear to God. They sent her to Old Earth."

"What?" Aton felt himself swaying. "Why?"

"I don't know."

Aton's rage bloomed like a flower. His hand clenched on the gun and it vibrated in his grip. The guard's eyes rolled up. He twitched and fell limp in his chair. His hands and feet trembled.

Aton turned and strode back to the Xest's cell. He started going through the keys, jamming them into the lock, barely aware of what he was doing.

The Xest was signing to him. "The Sergeant Self tells the truth."

Aton finally got the door open. He stopped. *How do you know?*

"Xest Self hears his thoughts before his dissolution with your weapon."

Not dissolution. He's just paralyzed for a short time.

The Xest signed regret. "In that case, this weapon cannot give dissolution to small Xest Self?"

No. Come on, we've got to get to your ship. Aton glanced around, saw the mini-Xest, picked it up, and put it in his pocket. The creature felt stiff and wiry, and was warm to the touch. It squirmed in his pocket as if trying to make itself more comfortable.

"Large Xest Self wishes to retrieve diplomatic documents."

Does Xest Self want to get chopped into little pieces?

"No!" The alien signed the word so emphatically, it almost dislocated its legs.

That's what'll happen if anyone catches you.

"Xest Self sees many human thoughts and knows all human selves on floors above are sleeping. Please wait." It ceased using its legs for sign language and scurried out of its cell. Aton watched helplessly as the alien ran to the door, lifted the latch with one leg, and went pattering up the stairs.

Aton followed, creeping slowly, all senses alert. He remembered clearly the way he'd been brought in. Faint light filtered up through the open door from the sergeant's oil lamp in the basement.

Aton paused in a passageway on the ground floor. Ahead of him was the door leading out to the yard at the back of the palace. There was a huge key in a wrought-iron lock; he turned it slowly. The door creaked inward on its hinges.

He heard a scurrying of many feet. The Xest appeared suddenly, a roll of papers clutched under one of its eight legs, the remaining seven pumping furiously. It hesitated long enough to sign to Aton, "Quickly! One human is now awake!"

Aton jerked the door open. Cool night air washed in.

The alien ran out into the darkness.

Heavy footsteps approached along the corridor. "Who's there?" A sleepy guard's voice.

Aton aimed the nerve gun at the shadowy figure and fired. He was just within range; the man gasped, stumbled, and fell.

Aton ran out of the door, following the Xest into the night. Just beyond the trees, the alien ship was a pointed black silhouette against the moonlit sky.

chapter vii _____

Aton opened his eyes to find Votnik kneeling over him, pressing with both hands on his chest. He shivered convulsively, rolled on his side, and coughed water out of his lungs.

"Easy, my friend. You're going to be all right."

Aton nodded weakly. He remembered being trapped in the water as the vortex dragged him down, holding him until he finally blacked out. It had only been for a few minutes, though it had felt like hours.

He managed to sit up. A torrent of water was roaring out of a hole in a sheer face of rock twenty feet away. It cascaded down into a pool and surged into a narrow channel beneath the stone shelf where Aton now found himself. From there, the river flowed on through the center of a long, wide, twisting tunnel whose roof was festooned with stalactites.

He saw Gwinnie sitting near his feet, wet clothes pasted to her thin body. It looked as if she and Votnik had hauled him out between the two of them. Oris was sitting on a boulder a short distance away, wringing water out of her long black hair. "What happened to Snyder?" Aton asked.

Oris gestured to the hole in the rockface. "He hasn't come through. He must be dead." She glared at Aton. "Why him, not you?"

"Easy, now," said Votnik. "This is not time to—"

Oris pointed her finger at Aton. "You killed Jacko!"

"No." Aton shook his head. "No, those animals, the apetiles, killed Jacko."

"You guessed how they'd react when you told him to throw that rock at the old man. You planned it."

Aton paused. He could deny the charge, and in another place, at a bygone time, he seemed to remember following that path—sacrificing a man and never admitting that his own life had been paid for by the death of another.

Yet now he felt different. He looked up at Oris. "There was only one way for any of us to survive back there," he said quietly. "Someone had to distract those animals long enough for the rest of us to escape over the wall."

"He admits it!" she cried, turning to Votnik and Gwinnie. "You hear this?"

"If I had done anything else," Aton persisted, "all of us would have been torn to pieces."

Gwinnie frowned. "You mean you really knew all along that the apetiles would—"

"Jacko was the strongest and had the best chance of scoring a hit." Aton studied Oris for a moment. "You know, I don't believe you really cared about him that much. I think you knew I was setting him up, even though you didn't see exactly how. You certainly didn't try to stop me. But maybe that's why you're taking it out on me now: to cover up the fact that you went along with the idea."

A tic worked at the side of her mouth. She seemed uncertain of how to answer him. Abruptly she turned away, hiding her face.

It was the first real sign of weakness he had seen in her. Exhausted as he was, shivering in his sodden clothes, he felt a little surge of elation. And yet he had prevailed not by a show of force but by admitting his own sins. Weakness had conquered strength.

"What I did was wrong," said Aton. "But there was nothing that would have been right. In any case, none of us here has clean hands. Otherwise we wouldn't have been sentenced to Chthon in the first place."

"Man has a point," Votnik said.

Oris stood up. She had recovered her self-control. "All right, let's think about what we should do now." She pushed her wet hair back from her face. "It seems obvious that there's no hope of getting back to the rest of our group."

"Wouldn't know how to begin to find 'em," Votnik agreed.

"So that leaves just the four of us. No food, no weapons, and no idea where we are." She paused. "Perhaps it's time for a prayer."

"Does anyone really believe that'll do any good?" Aton asked.

She glared at him. "What right do you have—"

Aton turned to Votnik. "Do you?"

He looked uncomfortable. "Well, ah, I've always said as I respect a religious faith." He glanced cautiously at Oris. "But personally speaking, I tend to put my faith in things I can see and touch. Now, I'm not saying that's a path *everyone* should follow—"

Aton looked at Gwinnie. "How about you?"

Their eyes met. "Well—"

"You think it makes any sense, praying to a planet?"

"I don't know. I mean, it's just something we do. I don't know if it makes sense, exactly."

Aton turned to Oris. "It was a good way to keep people like Jacko in line. And I'm sure it added to your status as a leader. But the situation has changed, hasn't it?"

Her fingers clenched, gripping the rock she was sitting on. "You're wrong," she said finally; but her voice lacked its usual conviction. "You don't understand—"

"Look!" Gwinnie interrupted.

A shape had appeared in the torrent gushing out of the rockface. It was Snyder's body, broken and mottled with blood. It splashed down into the pool, surfaced after a moment, then headed toward them in the river, face down and trailing streamers of red.

"He must have been trapped in there the last ten, fifteen minutes," said Votnik. "Poor bastard. May as well let him go."

"No." Aton dropped to his belly, wriggled forward, and reached for the corpse as it floated toward him. He grabbed it by the hair.

"He's dead!" Oris shouted. "Why can't you leave him alone?"

Aton shook his head. "We need him."

"What the hell for?"

"Food."

"You're a monster," she said as he hauled the bloody corpse out of the water. "You don't care about anyone or anything."

"Survival," Aton told her.

Votnik scrambled down to lend a hand, moving his bulk with surprising agility. "Seems to me, if you don't mind my saying so, we're in no position to be choosy," he told Oris.

Gwinnie was holding her face between her hands, staring at the dead body. "My god, look at his head! It's completely caved in!" She shuddered.

"All right, all right, let's just—calm down." Oris paced away a short distance, then back again. "None of us wants to have to eat human flesh."

"None of us has any choice," said Aton.

"How do you intend to do it? Rip him apart with your teeth?"

"Yes, if necessary."

"If you don't mind my saying so," said Votnik, "I may be able to help." He reached inside his tunic. "When the old man threw the knives down into the arena, I took the precaution of picking up one of them, before we went over the wall." He handed it to Aton.

Aton examined the blade. It was crudely forged and spotted with rust, but sharp enough to cut flesh. "You're a resourceful man," he said to Votnik.

He seemed pleased by the compliment. "I try, my friend. I try."

She glared at them. "All right, you two do what

you like." She walked away and sat down with her back to them.

"I guess, maybe, I'll go join her," said Gwinnie. "If you're going to do what I think you're going to do, I don't want to see it." She gave a forced smile, and retreated.

Aton looked at Votnik. "What about you?"

"I'll do whatever needs to be done."

"All right. It'll be easiest if we start cutting right away, before rigor mortis sets in. I don't want to risk damaging the knife, so we'll avoid bone and muscle and go for fat. It's probably easier to digest, raw, and has more calories."

"Start with the buttocks?" Votnik suggested.

"That's what I was thinking, yes."

They turned Snyder on his face. Votnik grabbed a handful of the man's pallid flesh and pulled it up, stretching the skin. Aton started sawing with the knife. Viscous blood oozed out of the wound.

"You all right?" Aton asked, when he'd sliced off one of Snyder's buttocks and laid it to one side. Votnik's expression was hard to read behind his beard.

"As well as can be expected. Shall I deal with the next one?"

"Thanks." Aton handed over the knife.

"You know, I've been thinking, my friend," Votnik said as he started cutting, "how unfortunate it would be if you turned out to be the sort who holds a grudge."

Aton looked up. "What?"

Votnik discreetly lowered his voice. "I mean, if

you were thinking of taking revenge on someone who'd mistreated you."

"You mean Oris?"

"Indeed." Votnik removed a slab of Snyder's flesh.

"I'm just biding my time," Aton said.

"No, my friend, you are not. You are defying her, undermining her authority, and for all I know, planning to dispose of her."

Aton hesitated. "Are you warning me, or what? Where do you stand?"

Votnik looked Aton in the eye. "I stand wherever is best at any particular moment. On your side, on her side, it really makes no difference. I do suggest, though, that we'll all do better by cooperating, instead of competing. If I were you, I would settle my differences peacefully." He cut a large chunk out of Snyder's thigh and dumped it on a nearby rock. He sighed. "I must confess, this work is upsetting my stomach. I'm going to have to take a short break." He nodded to Aton, stood up, and walked slowly away.

chapter viii _____

Aton sensed someone behind him and turned quickly. He found Oris watching him.

He stood up warily, leaving the knife in Snyder's flesh. "What do you want?"

"I came to see if you needed help." Her face was expressionless, and her voice was neutral. "Do you?"

He had been working on Snyder's corpse steadily for half an hour, slicing and stacking the chunks of meat. His arms were tired, and he was sick of the sight of skin and blood. He made room for her. "Go ahead."

She squatted down, picked up the knife, and continued cutting where he had left off.

"I thought you said cannibalism was too—monstrous, for you to deal with."

"I was upset about Jacko," she told him, without looking up.

"What is this—some kind of apology?"

"No." The word was loud and abrupt. She paused; then resumed working, as calmly as before. "It's an explanation. You were right to pull Snyder out of the river. I would have seen that if I'd been less emotional."

"Did Votnik tell you to come and say this?"

She hesitated, choosing her words. "He suggested I might have overreacted to you."

Aton nodded to himself. "And I guess you've had to accept that the situation is very different now from when you were in control of a couple dozen people."

Her face flickered with brief anger. "Yes, that's become clear enough."

He looked at her body, and remembered his frustration and humiliation when she had forced herself on him sexually. "Not long ago, you told me that sooner or later you'd make me submit to you."

"I don't remember saying that." Her tone was flat. "But if I did, maybe I was wrong." Methodically, she continued her work.

A little later, the four of them sat around Snyder's carcass and consumed what they could. The meat was cold and greasy, and too tough to chew. Aton and Votnik choked down several large lumps, Oris managed a couple of mouthfuls, but Gwinnie couldn't bring herself to eat any at all.

"Maybe you could drink some blood mixed with water," Votnik suggested. "Stands to reason that would be better than nothing. You surely need to sustain yourself."

"All right." She climbed down to the river and came back with water in her cupped hands.

"Don't watch," said Aton as he picked up a piece of flesh, held it over her outstretched palms, and squeezed it as hard as he could. The blood had started to coagulate, but some large gobs dripped out.

He used his finger to stir them into the water. "Now drink," he told her.

She raised her hands to her lips, but began coughing and retching after the first swallow. "I can't," she gasped.

"You're being ridiculous." Oris came over to her. "You've eaten raw animal meat often enough. This is no different."

Gwinnie looked into Oris's face. Something seemed to pass between the two women. "Please don't make me." Gwinnie's face contorted, and she started to cry. "Please, Oris—"

"Stop it!" Oris slapped her, hard.

Gwinnie pulled away. "Can't you just leave me alone? What does it matter, anyway? We're never going to get out of here. What does it matter whether we die next week or right now?"

"That's not true," Oris snapped. "We must be very close to the surface. We could be out of here in just a couple days from now."

"I don't think I believe that," Aton said quietly.

She turned on him. "Why not?"

"As I understand it, you've been on the hard trek for several weeks. And all that time, you've been climbing, taking any tunnel leading upward. Isn't that right? It seems to me, if you were going to reach the surface, you would have got there by now."

"What are you trying to say—that it doesn't exist?"

"I'm remembering more and more, about Chthon." He paused, looking from Oris to Gwinnie, then to Votnik. "I didn't mention this before. But I was on a hard trek myself, once. It was successful. I escaped. And before me there had been a man named Bedeker."

"Name rings a bell," said Votnik. "Seem to remember, some story, a legend—"

"You escaped from Chthon?" Oris's voice was heavy with sarcasm.

"Yes."

"And then what—you decided to come back?"

"I was brought back. When I regained consciousness in that small cave, just before you found me, Bedeker was bending over me, as if he'd just put me there."

Oris turned to Votnik. "Do you believe any of this?"

"I'm not sure as I know what to believe," said Votnik. "Seems to me, this is a man with a past. Seems to me, it was mighty peculiar, finding him the way we did. Hard to think of any kind of explanation that makes an ordinary kind of sense."

Oris turned back to Aton. "Originally, you told us you were alone."

"Yes, because I didn't know how to explain who Bedeker was, or where he came from."

"You mean you lied to us. That means maybe you're lying to us now."

He shook his head. "I'm telling you all I know. I remember that to escape from Chthon the first time, we followed signs that Bedeker had left carved in the rock. And all the signs pointed down."

"Down? How can *that* make sense?"

"I don't know."

She frowned at him. "I'm beginning to wonder if

you're entirely sane. Your memory certainly isn't worth much; it was your memory that told you there was a cave near here full of grass and flowers."

"Yes, and we found that exact place," Aton said calmly. "It had changed, since my memory of it. But it was there."

"I think maybe he's right, Oris," said Gwinnie.

"What?" Oris turned on her.

"I—just have a feeling about it, that's all." She avoided Oris's eyes. "I mean, we've kept on and on, trying it your way. Maybe it's time to try something different."

Oris was silent for a moment. Suddenly, strangely, she smiled. "All right. All right, why not. You want to try it his way, we'll do that." She turned back to Aton. "It shouldn't take very long to find out if you're as full of shit as you seem to be."

"And if I am, then we can go back to doing things your way."

She nodded, still smiling at him with no humor at all. "Yes."

"Well, now," said Votnik. "Well, I must say as how I admire two people who can settle their differences." He rubbed his hands together. "So what's the plan?"

"We should move on as soon as possible," said Aton. "We're still not far from the cave where the apetiles held us prisoner. The underground river can't be the only link; there must be tunnels that could give them access, here."

"You think they could come and find us?" Gwinnie's voice rose plaintively.

"Yes." He went over to Snyder's body. "I managed to peel a large area of skin off the back, here, to wrap the rest of the pieces of meat, so we can carry them with us. We don't have anything else to carry the meat in, except for our clothes, and we need them for warmth. Now, I also opened up his abdomen and took out the intestines." He bent over the edge of the rocks and reached down into the river. "I let them trail in the water, to clean them."

Oris shook her head. "No way are they edible."

"That's right." Aton coiled the thin brown tube around his arm. "But we can use them as a substitute for wire or rope, to make a snare, to catch other creatures. Remember, we have no real weapons." He pulled the little dagger out of the corpse, rinsed it in the river, then used it as a pin to close the sack he had made from Snyder's skin. "This is all we've got."

There was an uneasy silence. "Very well," said Votnik. "Let's start walking."

They followed the river as it flowed down through the winding tunnel. The hiss and roar of the water was constant, making it impossible to listen for any predators that might be pursuing them. Aton considered taking one of the paths that occasionally branched from the main one, just to gain a respite from the noise; but his instincts told him to stay with the river.

The tunnel grew gradually wider as they continued, and the river grew deeper, fed by other underground streams. Aton imagined launching a boat onto it and setting sail on a voyage forever downward, into the core of the planet. He fantasized that if he reached the very heart of Chthon, somehow all of his uncertainties would finally be resolved.

They had been walking for two hours when they came upon the apetile skeleton. From a distance it looked like a ruined piece of machinery, bones sticking up like curved metal struts, silhouetted black against the green lichen-glow. Then, as Aton approached, he saw it was the remains of one of the apetiles. The spine was a foot in diameter, fifteen feet long. The rib cage was large enough for a man to stand inside.

"I don't like to think we're still in their territory," said Gwinnie, staring at the huge round skull.

Aton shook his head. "I don't think we are. This one may have died because it strayed too far from home, and starved to death. I don't see any sign that anything killed it. The skull and bones are undamaged."

"Impressive brutes," said Votnik. "I can't help thinking there should have been some way we could have taken over from the old man back there, and have those creatures serving us, instead of him."

"Want to go back and try it?" Aton suggested.

"Oh, no. Much obliged, but no. Not my style of operation at all."

Aton tried to sense what was really in Votnik's head, behind his bonhomie and his florid mannerisms. "I guess you don't like sticking your neck out."

Votnik looked at him sharply. Then he shrugged. "Why deny it? An easy life, my friend, has always been my objective."

Aton surveyed the site. "I think we should camp here."

"Any special reason?" Oris asked.

"Yes. These bones have been picked clean. That means other animals have come to feed here—in which case, we have a chance of snaring one."

"Assuming it doesn't kill us first," said Oris.

"In Chthon, there is always that chance." He uncoiled the guts he had stripped from Snyder's body, tied a knot in one end, and threaded the other through to form a noose. "I'll put a piece of our meat inside the apetile skeleton, as bait, and hang this around it." He started rigging the trap. "We'll take turns to stand guard. If an animal takes the bait, the person on watch will have to pull this tight." He glanced around. "There's a big stalagmite on that shelf of rock, there; we can anchor the end of the rope to that."

"I'll take first watch," Votnik volunteered.

Aton nodded. "Good. I'll take second." He laid the rope of intestines carefully across the rocks, then looked around for a place to lie down and rest. He saw a ledge high up on the cavern wall. Anyone trying to climb up to it would almost certainly make enough noise to wake him.

"See you in a few hours," said Votnik, retreating to his vantage point.

Oris walked over to Gwinnie and put her hand on her shoulder. "Come on. Time to sleep."

Gwinnie stood up without saying anything, and the two women walked away, disappearing together behind a pile of boulders.

A little later, Aton lay on his back on the ledge he had chosen. He felt calm, even though the chances of survival still seemed virtually nonexistent. He had no rational explanation for his decision to head deeper into Chthon, but there was a sense of inevitability about it, as if he was following a series of steps in a plan. Somehow, he still felt certain, he was destined to survive.

He closed his eyes and methodically released the tensions in his muscles. He slipped into sleep—and dreamed again.

CHAPTER 7 _____

"One senses that you are still discontent," said the Xest, now speaking through a miniature translation vocalizer that it wore like a silver button embedded on one side of its globular body.

Aton looked at the alien sharply, disliking its ability to read his mind with such accuracy. "It's true, I'm not entirely happy," he said. Speaking was doubly unnecessary: in addition to being telepathic, the Xest was totally deaf. At the same time, verbalizing was a habit that helped Aton to focus his thoughts.

The Xest made some adjustment to the navigation controls and rotated on its seat so that most of its eyes faced Aton. "Is this unhappiness related to your two selves? That is of great philosophical interest. May I learn the complete details? You promised that we could discuss it at length."

"All right." Aton shifted uncomfortably in his seat. The furnishings of the ship were designed to fit Xest anatomy, and the chairs looked like large toadstools. Their cushions were concave, to accept the alien's ovoid body, and eight indentations around the rim allowed its legs to dangle.

"I grew up on Hvee, a simple pastoral world," be began, "with no idea that I was different from others around me. Then, when I was seven, I experienced an encounter with a beautiful woman in a forest glade. She gave me a book of poetry; she sang to me. She was like an enchantress." As he spoke, he vividly remembered his first meeting with Malice: every color, every scent.

"But now I sense anger," said the Xest.

"Yes, because although this—seductress—didn't say so, she was my mother. My father had always said my mother died when I was born, but that was a lie. You see, he had secretly visited the planet Minion, where he met her, and took her back with him to Hvee. She gave birth to me there, but left him shortly afterward."

"The word 'malice' is in your mind."

"That was her name. A Minionette is always named after some negative emotion. She's semitelepathic; but her emotions are inverted. She experiences pleasure only when her mate experiences anger, or anguish, that he inflicts on her. She is, in effect, a slave, begging for abuse. But at the same time, she enslaves her mate: she traps him with her beauty, her loyalty, and her love. She provokes him, then feeds off him. He must always be frustrated, for if he tries to hurt her, it gives her pleasure, but he cannot love her, for she feels love as pain so severe it can bring death."

"A strange culture indeed," the Xest responded. One of its legs pressed buttons on a console, and a screen lit up. "With your permission, I will encode this in my databases. How did this genetic oddity occur?"

"Minion was planned as a pleasure world for the decadent rich. Minionettes were genetically engineered to be courtesans, beautiful, subservient to a man's wishes, able to withstand physical abuse, and virtually ageless. But according to what Malice told me, the gene-splice contained coding errors, resulting in the pathological personality type that I've just described. The Federation Proscribed the planet, and it's remained in quarantine for the last three centuries."

"One moment." The Xest lifted itself off its stool and walked across the cabin. "The lesser Xest has become immobilized." It reached into the food preparation area, and plucked a small wriggling yellow shape from the mouth of a food dispensing tube. "The small self wishes to grow bigger," the Xest observed. "That is a proverb, in my race. A sad statement on the Xest condition. Xest are many; resources are few." It put the small Xest on the floor and set a little dish of lumpy gray paste in front of it. The creature began eating it eagerly.

"Does your smaller self have a name?" Aton asked.

"Of course. It shares my name."

"Oh. But I don't know what your name is."

"In the Xest race, one tends to be reluctant to make use of names. The connotations of individuality are embarrassing to the self. But if you wish, you may address me as Srndhi."

"Srndhi?" Aton tried to imitate the sound sequence.

"Since the Xest language is nonvocal, it is hard to tell if the verbalization is correct. But it can suffice."

"All right. And your—son—has the same name too?"

"With a different intonation. It is of little importance, since we share the same thoughts." The parent Xest returned to its stool. "Enough of names. There must be more to tell of your encounter with the woman Malice."

"I suppose there is. I didn't see her again until I was fourteen, when she made a second clandestine visit to my world. This time, she—played on my adolescent sexuality."

"Pressing together of lips," said Srndhi, seeing the image in Aton's mind.

He nodded, finding it hard, even now, to confront his own emotions. "But she immediately disappeared again. I became obsessed; I wasn't interested in any other women. When I was twenty-one I enlisted, purely so that I could go looking for her on other worlds. I wanted her as a lover. I had no idea she was my mother, until I found her, after four years of searching . . . and she told me."

The Xest closed its eyes thoughtfully. "She who is the mother is also the mate?"

"On Minion, a woman lives so much longer than her lover, she customarily remarries the son they produce, and the son that that marriage produces, and on through several generations. It's as if you, and your son, there, decided to join together to produce still another offspring."

"But we are already joined together. The cells remember." It paused. "Another old Xest saying." It turned back to the navigation console. "We have achieved FTL speed," it noted. "We will reach Old Earth within two standard days, if my calculations are correct. Will you feel a need for food?"

"I will. But do you have anything suitable?"

Srndhi consulted a data display. "I will instruct the support system with needs of your carbon-based life form. But I regret I have interrupted your explanation, which continues to be of great philosophical interest."

"There's not much more to tell. One thing I learned is that as a result of my Minion genes, I have a tendency toward violence. I want to hurt those I love."

"But if you are to love a Minionette, then she would enjoy the hurt," the Xest observed.

"I can't live like that. It's pathological."

Srndhi paused as if thinking deeply. "One respectfully suggests that the path to contentment depends on acceptance of one's self."

"Is that another old Xest saying?"

"No, that is my own thought on your situation. But one thing is still unclear: how you and the woman Malice came to be on the planet Minion at this time."

"She suggested we spend a couple of days there. I agreed; I wanted to see my cultural heritage, if you can call it that. It was only a diversion. But while we were there—" He stopped speaking and remembered the violent scene in the village square.

Srndhi saw the pictures in Aton's mind. "You caused the dissolution of Human Selves."

Aton nodded.

"In my culture, that too is a crime, for dissolution

should be a voluntary act. Yet it causes little guilt, and the penalties are not severe."

A red light flashed in the food preparation area, and a dish emerged from a slot. "The meal is ready," said the Xest.

Aton retrieved the dish. Like the one that had been placed in front of the small Xest, it was piled generously with lumpy gray paste.

"The composition is quite different," Srndhi assured him.

"I hope so." Aton found a spoon that had a socket at one end, suitable for a Xest's leg. He scooped a sample of the paste, and found that it was totally tasteless.

"The human obsession with preserving life," the Xest went on, "is a far greater crime than your act negating it."

"It is?"

Srndhi stood up and paced to and fro, its eight limbs moving restlessly. "Your race is blind to the concept of debt. Already Human Selves are spread through one-third of the galaxy. Is there no end to this growth?"

"There are still a lot of empty worlds," Aton pointed out.

"It is my motive, as ambassador and sociobiologist, to understand this human need to multiply, and argue for its restraint. For this reason, I am pleased to travel to Old Earth, which is still the center of human political administration." It paused. "I am motivated also out of sense of obligation to you, for my release from the Minion prison, and aversion of the catastrophe of my subdivision into many hundred parts, incurring intolerable debt. Therefore, as a personal matter, I will endeavor to reunite your self with the Minionette, since I discern that the consequent fission of selves will eliminate the discontent of which you complain."

Aton smiled grimly. "You really think so?"

"It is clear from your innermost thoughts."

Aton spooned more of the paste. He nudged aside the small Xest, which was begging for scraps. "I appreciate your gesture," he said. "But the Earth system is large and highly developed, and we have no idea where Malice was taken, or even why."

"Not so!" The Xest activated a printing device, which exuded a sheet of flimsy yellow plastic covered in white hieroglyphics. "This transcript is of radio traffic recorded automatically by this transit vehicle while I was detained on Minion. There is an item, here: transmission to Earth from Minion via tachyon beam, shortly before our departure, stating that the Minionette Malice was placed in a coded ship—that is, one with locked navigation coordinates—to transport her to the Lunar Genetic Laboratories, 'as requested.' "

"Does it say why she was sent, or who the request was from?"

"No."

Aton stood up and walked to one of the viewports. Outside was featureless darkness; FTL transit was beyond normal spacetime. He imagined meeting Malice again. He had run with the Xest to its ship primarily to escape death on Minion; he had not expected to be able to pursue the Minionette. It had been Srndhi, reading Aton's thoughts and wishing to repay him, who had selected a course for Old Earth.

Aton turned away. "Is there somewhere I could lie down? It's been a long time since I had any rest."

"My Xest bed is regrettably not suitable."

Aton imagined some sort of padded bowl, and decided the alien was undoubtedly correct.

"However," Srndhi went on, "there is a Meditation Room, of qualities to induce great serenity. Would you please follow me?"

It led the way out of the control room, and Aton followed.

CHAPTER 8 _____

"One tires of receiving data by the mind," Srndhi explained, opening a door and gesturing with one of its legs for Aton to walk through. "At such times the Meditation Room provides relaxation. Also, enlightenment."

It was a small circular chamber containing no furniture or ornamentation of any kind. The walls and ceiling glowed white. The floor was black, and yielded under Aton's feet as he stepped onto it. "I'm not quite sure I understand," he said.

"It becomes a burden always to listen to other selves, reports from ship systems, and so on. This room is shielded, providing solitude."

"Like a sensory deprivation chamber," Aton said. "But since I lack telepathic abilities, it's of no special benefit to me."

"True. However, as well as screening one's mind from input, the room receives one's own mental output, and responds most therapeutically. Please lie down."

Aton shrugged. "If you say so." He stretched out on the cushioned floor.

"Whenever you feel a wish to leave, the chamber will release you," the Xest said. It extended one leg, forming the galactic sign of friendship, then retreated and closed the door.

The room was totally silent and pleasantly warm. Aton stared up at the featureless white ceiling. His mind wandered, and for some reason, after a while, he remembered lying in bed one summer on Hvee, when he was five years old.

The image of his childhood bedroom became clear in his mind—and then he saw it, like a three-dimensional photograph, reproduced on the ceiling above his head. The walls darkened and the ceiling brightened, and the meditation room recreated the picture in every detail.

It soon became much more than a mere echo of his thoughts. As he watched, the image underwent a metamorphosis. The walls of his childhood bedroom curved in and faded to a pastel color, like the petals of a Hvee flower. He was enclosed in the flower; and then it burst open, expelling him into a dark sky.

He felt overwhelmed by an angry sense of loss, of innocence stolen from him. He was floating like a grain of dust, across a ruined landscape—the green hills of Hvee turned brown and dead, ravaged by some plague. Suddenly he realized that he was the plague: he was a virus, a carcinogen, destroying all forms of life.

The contours of the landscape became a huge face: his own face, dark and grim. The skin shrank and grew wrinkled, like paper shriveling and blackening in a fire. Then it flaked away, and blood poured out.

But this was not his blood. The crimson flowed over soft, pale skin—the naked form of Malice, lying on a bed of Hvee flowers, bleeding from a dozen vicious lacerations. Aton saw himself standing over her, wielding the Initiator's whip. She was arching her back, turning her face to one side, her eyes sparkling, her cheeks flushed, her lips parted in ecstasy.

The whip cut across her thighs, the skin opened, and she sighed and smiled.

The whip cut across her breasts, and the pink nipples became stained with red. She threw her head back and laughed. His anger, his torment, his sadism, were a source of amusement, nothing more.

He threw the whip aside and grabbed her. He tore her flesh from her body, and still she laughed, her green eyes mocking him.

He saw himself collapse between her thighs, crying helplessly. She loomed over him. Her skin had healed, her perfection was restored. She was suddenly five times his size, lifting him with casual ease, placing him between her soft, naked breasts. He wriggled and screamed, a helpless infant. She reached for his little penis and toyed with him.

He tried to pull away—but his skin had become fused with hers. Her body was assimilating him. He was sinking into her flesh, becoming engulfed by her femininity.

With a furious wrench, he broke free—and found himself floating in sudden darkness. There was nothing, now, but the stars, lifeless and uncaring. He was alone, and the emptiness inside him was like the emptiness of space itself.

A sudden spray of silver particles burst across the dark panorama, each one a metal capsule containing human life. One of the capsules drifted into close-up, and he saw through its shell to the interior. Men and women, nestled together like fetuses in a womb.

The capsule became a glowing meteor, trailing fire. It impacted on a planet, split open, and humanity burst out. The flesh-colored forms doubled, then quadrupled in number. They merged with the planet's green ecology, permeated it, then dominated it.

The fantasy images became scrupulously detailed. They were being created not just from Aton's own mind, now, but from some immense hidden database in the Xest ship.

Aton watched as humanity conquered the alien world. Years became seconds; he saw the eradication of alien species, the destruction of an ecosystem, its replacement by a human monoculture.

Another world: another swarm of humanity. But these were genetic freaks, breathing methane through bulbous vents in their chests. Their skin had a gray metallic sheen, and their eyes were covered with membranes—sealed against the corrosive atmosphere.

Other mutants moved across Aton's field of view: a parade of misfits modified to subsist on countless planets. There were women whose babies were born inside leathery protective eggs; fish-men with gills in their necks, webbing joining their arms to the bodies; hermaphrodites with short, stumpy limbs that could withstand a world of high-gravity where they walked on all fours. . . .

And somewhere, almost lost among these spawning hordes, Aton saw Malice and himself.

The river of humanity spread out to fill the galaxy, yet it sprang from just one source. The picture shifted. The stream of mutant human forms was shown emanating from an egg-shaped dome. Aton realized he must be looking at the Lunar Genetic Laboratories. Here, for centuries, colonists had been tailor-made for survival on other worlds.

Aton wrenched himself free, mentally, from the images in front of his eyes. The tachyon message that Srndhi had intercepted had stated that Malice was being transported to these same laboratories. Aton formed a demand in his mind: to see inside the installation that was pictured in front of him.

The meditation room responded. The dome loomed closer, till it filled his view. But there it stopped. No door opened, and the outer walls remained obstinately opaque.

Evidently there were limits to the data stored in the Xest ship's computer. It could not show him something that neither he, nor it, had seen.

Aton felt a sudden need to escape from the room. Immediately, the image on the ceiling faded to white, and the walls brightened. He found himself lying on the floor, blinking. He looked toward the door, and it opened silently.

A few minutes later, he returned to the control room. Srndhi turned to greet him and eyed him sagely for a moment, sampling Aton's thoughts.

"Your self finds enlightenment," it commented finally.

"I—think so." Aton sat down. He looked around, his vision still colored by the images of life and death. "You were right. It was—enlightening."

"For a long time my race has chosen to remain distant from yours," Srndhi said. "We have conducted trade with humans, but have discouraged other contact, finding it somewhat . . . unpleasant. Please do not take offense; as a nontelepathic being, it is difficult for you to understand."

Aton nodded.

"My task was to visit worlds colonized by humanity," the Xest continued, "to assemble the data as evidence, and present to the human Federation our request for restricted growth." Srndhi paused. "This is what I must do, when we reach the moon. What, now, are your plans?"

"I have to find Malice. The images in the meditation room proved to me that I can't leave that situation unresolved."

The Xest waved its legs in a signal of concern. "There is nothing more that you feel a need to do?"

"Your motives and mine are different, Srndhi. But they can overlap. It seems to me, your ultimate aim is to reduce suffering and restore balance. In a different sense, that also could be my motive too. We can assist each other. Look into my mind."

And he visualized the plan he had devised.

chapter ix _____

This time, the dream-memories fell quickly from his mind. He woke suddenly, sitting up, his pulse beating fast. The cave was echoing with sounds: a high-pitched guttural screaming, like the cry of a huge bird, and a slapping noise, as if some giant hand were striking wet flesh.

Aton peered down from his vantage point. There was something large and ugly in the snare he had laid, shrieking in anger and blundering around, its body smacking against the rocks. Stretched out beside it was a second shape, hard to distinguish in the dim lichen-glow.

Aton scrambled down and started running. "Votnik!" he shouted.

As he came closer he saw the large bearded man lying on his back, being trampled by the creature. It looked like a huge sea lion, fifteen feet or more in length, with a shiny black body tapering to two fins at the tail. The resemblance ended there, however. Four stumpy, vestigial legs protruded from the body, terminating in long claws that scrabbled ineffectually at the ground. The creature's head was bulbous, and it had a long, tapering snout, horny and pointed, like a huge beak.

It was squirming, trying to free its neck from the noose that Aton had laid. It pawed Votnik's body, crisscrossing his skin with bloody claw marks.

"What's happening?" Gwinnie came running out from behind the heap of boulders where she had been with Oris.

"Help me get him out," Aton shouted to her.

"Is he dead?"

"I don't know." He flinched away as the animal lunged at him, screaming. "See if we can grab his legs."

Her eyes were round with fear. "I don't think I can—"

"Come on!" He ducked down, seized Votnik by one of his ankles, and heaved. The man was heavy; his bulk barely moved. Gwinnie gave a little cry of fear, but joined him. Together they pulled the man free, just as the snared creature turned on them again, its beak snapping angrily.

Aton checked Votnik's vital signs.

"What the hell is going on?" Oris came striding toward him. She was naked, pulling on her convict clothes as she walked. He caught a brief glimpse of her firm, high, dark-nippled breasts, her narrow waist, her powerful thighs.

"Votnik's dead," Aton told her flatly.

Her face remained expressionless. She glanced at the man's body, then at the creature in the trap. "If that thing gets loose, it'll kill us all."

"We'd better run," Gwinnie quavered. She started

edging backward, looking from Oris to Aton as if for reassurance.

Aton shook his head. "We need it for food."

"All right," said Oris, "give me the knife."

He hesitated. Their eyes met. "No," he said. He turned and walked around the creature, circling it and waiting till its head pointed away from him. Then he leaped forward, onto its back.

The skin was rough, thick, and not as slippery as it looked. Aton wrapped his left arm around and under the creature's neck, and slashed the knife into its right eye.

It bucked under him and tossed him off. He landed painfully on the rocks and scrambled clear as it tried to grab him with its front feet. Claws scraped inches from his shoulder.

He got up. "Make a noise," he shouted to Oris and Gwinnie. "Get its attention."

Gwinnie screamed shrilly. Oris picked up a rock and threw it at the animal's head.

It turned toward them, its wounded eye leaking colorless fluid streaked with blood. Aton switched the knife to his other hand, jumped forward, slashed the left eye, and jumped back.

The creature's screeching changed to a tormented howl as it wriggled to and fro, totally blind now.

"It's going to break free," Gwinnie wailed.

"Can we crush it with a rock?" said Oris.

Aton shook his head. "It's too big, too tough." He glanced around and saw the apetile skeleton nearby, big bones scattered across the rocks. He selected one that was was six feet long, six inches thick at one end, pointed at the other. "Help me," he called to the two women.

Together, the three of them lifted it up. "It's not sharp enough to stab through its skin," said Oris.

"No. But it'll fit down its throat. Wait till it turns this way."

The blinded creature heard Aton's voice. It slithered around, its stumpy little legs trying to find a foothold on the rocks. It opened its beak in another high-pitched howl.

"Now."

Together, the three of them thrust forward. The tip of the big, curved bone rammed into the seal-creature's gaping mouth. "Deeper!" Aton shouted, and they pushed hard, sliding the bone in.

It made throttled, gargling noises and writhed violently, almost wrenching the bone free from their grasp.

"Deeper!" Aton shouted again. He pushed forward, his bare feet slipping on the wet rocks. The bone slid further, stabbing down into the animal's stomach. Its struggles intensified, and it waved its front legs futilely.

Aton backed away. "Just a matter of time, now," he said. He wiped sweat from his forehead. He realized his hands were trembling.

"Could take hours for it to die," said Oris.

Aton shook his head. "It doesn't have gills, and I don't see a blowhole in its head or back. It must breathe through its mouth, in which case it'll suffocate."

Oris studied the beast calmly, as if its shuddering

and muffled keening noises were just mildly interesting. She turned back to Aton. "It seems you're right," she agreed.

"You ever see one of those things before?" Aton asked her.

"Never."

"I don't think I ever did, either. Fish with legs. Legfish."

Gwinnie sat down heavily. "This is just so awful. All this violence and death."

Aton said nothing. He walked over to Votnik and examined the man again. The scratches from the claws of the legfish were superficial, still oozing red, but there were dark bruises and a deep puncture wound in his chest that had obviously killed him. The blood in it had already darkened and dried at the edges.

Aton glanced back toward where Votnik had stood watch. There were some faint scuff marks in the rocks, as if there had been a struggle. He turned toward the river, and saw a wet trail where the legfish had heaved itself out and crawled to the trap, attracted by the bait.

"We should bury him," said Gwinnie.

"In what?" Oris's voice was scornful.

"It's true," said Aton. "There aren't even enough loose rocks to build a cairn over him. The best we can do is put him in the river."

"Or just leave him," said Oris.

Aton shook his head. "I don't want to do that."

She treated him to her strange, thin smile. "So you have a sentimental streak, after all."

Aton stared at her levelly. "Votnik was a good man."

"Sometimes, he was. Other times, he was a devious, deceitful son-of-a-bitch."

Aton sighed. "I'm not interested in arguing. Are you going to help me?"

"Sure, why not?" She bent down and grabbed the man's legs.

Aton paused for a moment as if trying to read Oris's intentions. Then he turned and took hold of Votnik's wrists. Together, they dragged him to the edge of the river.

Aton took a last look at Votnik's face. "Live and let live," he murmured. Angrily, then, he pushed the body over the edge. It rolled, splashed into the water, and started drifting swiftly downstream.

He stayed alone by the river for a while, staring at the water without really seeing anything. Vague memories tugged at him, half formed and tantalizing. He recalled hunger and death on the last hard trek he had made. Some convicts, like Votnik, had been ripped apart by Chthonic beasts. Others, he was sure, had been killed by their fellowmen.

Aton looked down at his hands. He couldn't be sure, but he suspected that he himself had shared in the killing.

He bent over the river, and saw his reflection. The face looked disturbingly—different. The hair and beard were darker than he remembered. The eyes looked younger. "Everything here is wrong," he murmured. "It's all—inverted, from the way I remember it."

"This thing is dying," Oris's voice called from

behind him. "You want to bring that knife over here? We'll start cutting it up."

Aton turned away from the river.

Aton skinned the creature's tail, and they ate its raw meat. It was moist and tender, like uncooked fish, and needed little chewing. Each of them had second and third helpings, and a sense of well-being grew inside Aton for the first time since he had originally woken and found himself in Chthon.

He watched as Gwinnie relaxed, and even Oris seemed to lose some of her habitual cold control. At the same time, however, there was a new underlying tension. With Votnik gone, the dynamics of the group had changed.

"So what's your plan now?" Oris asked, after the three of them had sat quietly for a while. Her voice sounded lazy, but her eyes seemed alert, gleaming in the dim green light.

"No different from before." Aton made his voice deliberately casual.

"You want to dump the rest of Snyder's . . . re-mains, pack as much of this meat as we can carry, and walk on?" There was a feline quality about her, like a large cat that had just eaten, but would soon be hungry again.

"I've been thinking of an alternative," Aton said. "If I skin the rest of the legfish, and do the job right, we'll have a large piece of hide, maybe ten feet by fifteen. We can use its guts as rope to lash together some of the bones from the apetile skeleton, then stretch the hide across them, and make a boat." Once again he was seeing his fantasy image of a long voyage down into the center of Chthon.

"Very interesting," said Oris. She yawned, stretched, and lay back, clasping her hands behind her head. Her breasts moved under the thin cloth of her tunic. She lifted one knee, carelessly exposing the inner side of her thigh. "Don't you think that's interesting, Gwinnie?" she asked, without looking away from Aton's face.

"Uh, yes, sure." The younger woman nodded quickly.

"See? Gwinnie seems to like the idea," said Oris. "So I guess that's a majority vote, and we should always do what the majority wants. Isn't that right, Aton?"

Aton stood up. "I'll get to work," he said shortly, and turned away.

chapter x _____

The animal skin had a rank, fishy odor and was slimy on the underside, making it difficult to grasp and peel away from the flesh beneath. It took Aton a couple of hours to detach the hide in one piece, and then he started building a wide, shallow framework of bones to support it. The result would be a dish-shaped boat just large enough to contain the three of them.

The edges of the skin now needed to be attached to the rim of the framework. Aton used the knife to punch holes at intervals, then threaded fishgut through them, winding it around in a spiral stitch. His hands were bruised and aching from skinning the legfish, and the gut kept slipping through his fingers.

"Gwinnie can finish that for you," said Oris. She had helped with the work in a desultory way, holding the carcass while Aton skinned it. Mostly, though, she had stood back and given curt instructions to Gwinnie, who had obeyed without comment or protest.

"Do you think your hands are strong enough?" Aton asked the girl.

"I'll try." She flashed him a shy smile.

He gave her a pointed stone that he had been using to force the gut through the slits in the hide. "Careful," he told her. "If you push too hard, the rock will slip and cut the skin."

As he spoke, it happened. She gave a little cry of dismay and sat back, sucking a bruised finger.

Oris walked over. "Didn't you hear what he told you, Gwinnie?" she said.

"I was doing my best." She looked tired and pale, and sounded plaintive.

Oris put her hand under Gwinnie's chin and tilted her head up. "Your best wasn't much good, was it?" She moved her hand behind the girl's head, curled her fingers in her hair, and tugged, making Gwinnie wince.

"Please, Oris, I—"

"Quiet. I'm tired of your whining. You think you deserve special treatment, is that it?" She tugged harder on Gwinnie's hair, till tears came to her eyes.

"No, Oris."

Oris released her abruptly. "Go wait for me over there." She pointed to the heap of boulders where they had slept together.

Gwinnie got up without a word. Her shoulders were slumped, and she seemed to be on the verge of tears.

"That wasn't necessary," Aton said quietly.

"It's none of your business," Oris told him. She was breathing quickly, as if the little scene had aroused her.

"There's only three of us now," Aton pointed out.

"Anything you do that affects one of us, affects me too. That makes it my business."

She moved closer to him, till she was looking into his eyes from just a couple of feet away. "Some people are weak, and some people are strong. I don't do anything to Gwinnie that she doesn't want me to do. But I don't have to explain myself to you." She turned and walked away, following Gwinnie behind the rocks.

Aton stood for a minute, listening. He heard faint voices, but couldn't distinguish the words.

He went back to work on the boat, painstakingly threading the gut through each slit and wrapping it around the bone rim beneath. But he found it hard to concentrate.

Finally, he crept across the cave and started climbing the heap of boulders. He moved silently, taking care not to dislodge any small stones that would rattle down and betray his presence. He breathed quietly through his open mouth and paused frequently to listen. After a few minutes he reached the top, peered down the other side, and saw them.

Oris was sitting naked on the floor of the cave, with her shoulders propped against the stones behind her. Her knees were pulled up, and her legs were spread apart. Gwinnie was kneeling in front of her, with her head bowed and her arms hanging limply by her sides.

"Kiss my feet, now," Oris was instructing her.

Gwinnie shuffled backward, bent down, and did as she was told.

"Very good." Oris's voice was gently mocking.

"My stomach, now. Come on!" She grabbed Gwinnie's hair and jerked her forward. The girl lost her balance and fell, banging her face against a rock.

"Clumsy little bitch." Oris reached down under Gwinnie's body and Gwinnie cried out in pain. "Now do what I just told you."

Awkwardly, Gwinnie bent her head and kissed the other woman's belly.

"Higher, now. My breasts. Do you hear me?" Gwinnie whimpered again, then obeyed. "That's better." Oris's voice softened to a caress. "Very good, Gwinnie. Good girl." She stroked her hair. "My little slave girl."

Aton retreated, preferring not to watch any more. He climbed back down to the floor of the cave.

He went back to work on the boat and focused all his attention on the job. Half an hour went by; and then he heard footsteps padding toward him across the rocks.

He looked up and saw Gwinnie standing there, shy and self-conscious. "I've come back to help you. I'll try harder not to mess it up this time."

Aton frowned. "Did Oris tell you to do that?"

Gwinnie nodded.

Aton stood up. "How about you? What do you want to do?"

She avoided his eyes. "I want to help, like I just said."

"Then go ahead." He gestured for her to take over, where he had almost finished the job.

She worked with determination, and threaded the

gut neatly through several holes, pulling it tight around the frame.

Then she stopped and and glanced quickly over her shoulder to make sure they were alone. "Aton?"

He squatted beside her. "What is it?" he asked. Looking at her face, he remembered the way he had seen her being forced to kiss Oris's feet. He felt himself becoming insistently, perversely aroused, and he shook his head, wanting to get rid of the memory.

"Will you—watch out for me?" Her voice was a whisper.

"What do you mean?"

"Oris gets—mad sometimes. And now there's only me for her to be mad at."

"You mean you want me to keep her away from you?"

"Oh no!" Gwinnie's eyes widened for a moment. "No. Just, if things ever get really out of hand. I mean, if you ever hear me cry for help—"

He nodded. "All right."

"Thanks." She flashed him a brief smile, then turned her head quickly, hiding her face from him.

"Is she doing it right this time?" Oris came up behind Aton, striding with a confident swagger.

"She's doing fine," Aton said.

"I finished it." Gwinnie knotted the end of the gut.

Oris went and inspected the job. "I knew she could handle it. She just needed the right kind of incentive." She turned and pinched Gwinnie playfully on the cheek. "Right?"

Gwinnie pulled away. She didn't answer.

"You two were so quiet over here," Oris went on,

"I wondered what you were up to." She smiled, showing her teeth. "I thought maybe Aton was making a pass at you, Gwinnie. Was that what he was doing? Putting his hands on you?"

Gwinnie took a deep breath. She summoned her strength to confront Oris. "Look, I don't—"

"Just answer the question."

Gwinnie clenched her fists. She bit back whatever she had been going to say. "No. He didn't try to touch me."

Oris grasped the hem of Gwinnie's tunic and jerked it up in one swift motion, revealing the other woman's body. "I can't understand why not," she said. She turned to Aton. "Look at that. Wouldn't you want to touch a body like that? Those soft thighs, those cute little breasts?"

"Oris!" Gwinnie's voice was shrill. She wrenched free and pulled the tunic down. She ran a hand through her disheveled hair. "Stop it!"

"Stop what, Gwinnie?"

"Just *stop!*"

"I think it's time to get this boat into the river," Aton said deliberately. "Are you two going to help me, or shall I drag it on my own?"

There was a long pause. Oris stared at Gwinnie, as if imagining what she would like to do to her. Finally, she shrugged and turned away. "All right," she said to Aton. "Why not?"

"Gwinnie, can you get the other side?"

She recovered her composure, bit by bit. "Sure." She moved quickly, avoiding looking at either of them.

It took all their strength to haul the boat to the river and turn it over. It flopped down into the water with a big splash, and Aton had to grab it to stop it from drifting away downstream.

"Can you fetch the rest of the meat?" Aton called to Gwinnie. "And the knife. And maybe a couple small bones from the apetile skeleton; they might be useful for something."

"All right." She hurried away, seeming glad to have something to do.

Oris stepped into the boat. It rocked under her. "The skin still stinks," she complained.

Gwinnie hurried back, handed Aton the knife, and dumped a heap of legfish meat into the bottom of the boat. She went back for more, and finally added a couple of bones. Then she stepped in, placing her feet on the frame of the boat, careful not to put her weight on the hide stretched across it.

Aton stepped sat down opposite the women, then pushed the boat away from the shore. It started drifting swiftly downstream.

Most of the time, the current held them in the center of the river. Only when the channel curved did the sides of the boat rub briefly against the banks; and then they sailed onward again, moving relentlessly down the tunnel.

Aton lay staring upward at the glowing patches of green on the roof of rock moving past, and he listened to the river lapping against the animal hide beneath him. He reached for another piece of legfish meat, and chewed it slowly.

"We're moving faster than before," said Oris. She was lying opposite, one arm draped loosely around Gwinnie's shoulders, as if claiming her.

"That's right," Aton agreed.

"And you don't really know where it's taking us, do you?"

"I just know that this was the right thing to do," he answered her. "I have some vague memories—"

"They always are vague, aren't they?"

Aton frowned. "How about yours? Are any of your recollections sharp and clear? I noticed no one in your group ever talked about the past. No one even mentioned life in the garnet mines, before you started your hard trek."

"My memories are clear enough."

"Then tell me how long you've been in Chthon, and what the tunnel looked like that brought you down from the surface, and the name of the Federation officer who arrested you, for whatever crime you committed."

There was a long silence. "None of that matters."

"How about you, Gwinnie?"

The girl frowned. She glanced uneasily at Oris. "I'm—not sure. I mean, there are things I think I remember, but when I try to get the pictures in my head, I can't tell what's real and what isn't."

"It doesn't prove anything," Oris snapped. "All it proves is that being down here drives people crazy. If we ever get out, I'll have no problems. That I'm sure of." She turned away from him, folded her arms under her breasts, and closed her eyes.

Aton watched her for a long while, till her breathing became slow and regular. He was desperately tired himself. He leaned forward and beckoned for Gwinnie to do the same. "Can you stay awake?" he whispered.

"I think so," she whispered back.

"You stand watch, then. Push us away from the bank, if necessary. If anything else happens, shout."

She nodded.

Aton lay back. He carefully slipped the dagger behind him, so that no one could reach it without waking him.

The boat rocked gently, and the sounds of the river soothed him. Within moments, he drifted into sleep.

This time, as consciousness slipped away, he seemed to hear a voice telling him he was coming closer, now, and soon he would arrive. He tried to ask what he was approaching, and what would happen to him; but he found he couldn't speak—couldn't even breathe—and then the voice was gone and he was dreaming again, of events distant in space and time.

CHAPTER 9 _____

The moon was a cream-colored crescent stippled with shadow, hanging against the misty sprawl of the Milky Way. Aton stared out of the viewport and realized that the journey was almost over.

He turned to Srndhi. "Still no contact?"

The Xest was on its stool at the control panel. "Correct. There is no response."

"Since your race took the trouble to place an embassy on the moon, I should have thought they'd maintain regular communications with it."

"Of course." Srndhi descended from its stool and moved around the small room, flexing its legs. "One has stayed in touch with Ambassador Twnde over the years. Unfortunately, its reports started to become erratic some time ago."

"Maybe you should have sent a replacement."

The Xest paused in front of Aton. "You do not understand the circumstances. When our two races met each other more than a century ago, Xests decided there was little to be gained from contact with humans. At that time, with respect, they felt humanity was . . . distasteful."

"Because of our policy of expansion?"

"That was not then so obvious. What disturbed my people was your lack of, ah, mental etiquette. Humans constantly broadcast their thoughts without discretion or modesty. For most Xests, this cacophony creates considerable mental stress."

"I didn't realize." Aton shrugged uncomfortably. "But I guess there's not much I can do about it."

Srndhi gestured with a foreleg. "We do not hold humans responsible, any more than you would blame a deaf person for talking incoherently because he cannot hear himself. The point, though, is that being an ambassador on a human world is an act of great risk and bravery. Twnde insisted on volunteering. He felt our races needed to understand one another, and of course he was correct. Over the years, however, his solitary situation, bombarded by thousands of human minds, seems to have caused him to become . . . unwell."

"You mean he's on the moon *alone*? No staff, no helpers?"

"He insisted on that. The debt—"

"Yes, of course, the debt. But how long as he been there?"

Srndhi twitched a leg vaguely. "Eighty of your years, perhaps." It turned back to the control panel.

"Eighty years? Incredible. But can't you make ordinary telepathic contact?"

"One's telepathic range is limited to around five hundred feet. Otherwise, one would hear the whole galaxy screaming." Srndhi shuddered at the thought.

Aton walked over to the control panel. He looked

down at a series of colored levers. There were no data displays; Srndhi seemed to receive input by direct mental contact with the ship's computer. "So how do you communicate at long range? Obviously you don't use radio or tachyon transmission."

"Indeed no. One's equipment amplifies, modulates, receives, and transmits the pure telepathic function. But one prefers not to discuss it further. It is a proprietary technology."

"You mean, you don't want humans getting in on it and fouling the mental waveband."

"Reluctantly, one must agree that you speak the truth."

Aton laughed sourly. "You really think we're contemptible, don't you?"

Srndhi waved its legs in agitation. "One has learned that for humans, the individual is separate from the species. A most strange concept, but it is so. Therefore I do not judge you by humanity as a whole."

"Yeah? So you might say, some of your best friends are humans."

Srndhi paused thoughtfully. "That may be overstating the case," it responded. "But in principle—"

"All right, all right, it was a joke," said Aton. "Forget about it. We should be thinking ahead. If Twnde's dead, how are we going to follow our plan?"

"Not dead. One senses the mental presence." The Xest gestured to his controls. "But it does not respond. Perhaps when in closer contact with my Xest consciousness, it will revive. One cannot tell. But wait, we are receiving a transmission."

Aton waited impatiently as the Xest lapsed silent,

in mental communion with its ship. "A conventional radio transmission only," it explained after a moment. "Luna control has assigned us a landing bay. They are guiding us down." The ship started turning gently as it spoke. "Do not be concerned. Our artificial gravity will compensate." It snapped a series of switches. Through the viewport, the sunlit crescent of the moon rotated slowly as the ship moved toward orbital injection.

"So when we land," said Aton, "we'll try to find Twnde, your ambassador, and see if he's in any condition to assist us."

"Correct. One hopes you will be of great help in locating the embassy."

"Me? But I told you, I've never been on Luna before. The Old Earth system is a backwater. Everyone says it's a sleazy, run-down sector; even tourists don't come here anymore."

"Yes. Yes, one's own data confirms this." Srndhi opened a compartment in the control panel and shuffled through a stack of documents. "But there are some aids, here. A map, supplied by Twnde some decades ago. And negotiable currency." It lifted a small box between two of its legs, and offered it to Aton. "Please take custody. Even though the territory is unfamiliar, it will be easier for you, a human, to comprehend it."

Aton squinted at the map, then accepted the box. It was surprisingly heavy. "What's in here?"

"Highly refined gold."

"Gold? But this isn't a backwater planet like Minion, this is—"

"Nevertheless," Srndhi interrupted, "gold is their currency. Surely, you recall your Earth history. Original moon colonists, four hundred years ago, described themselves as libertarians."

"I remember something about that. What of it?"

"They were entrepreneurs. They rejected most forms of government. Their only concern was individual liberty, and creating wealth. For reasons one finds unclear, they distrusted electronic credit or even paper currency, and insisted that transactions be paid with gold. An idiosyncracy that persists today, out of nostalgia, perhaps."

"Strange," said Aton.

Srndhi became motionless for a moment, locked in another mental exchange with its ship. "Final descent," it said to Aton. "Please seat yourself. Soon the artificial gravity must be canceled. A slight bump, nothing more." Its legs moved in complex patterns across the control panel.

Aton sat down and held on to the edge of his stool with both hands. He watched through the nearest viewport as the lunar landscape came into focus, dusty seas spotted with jagged rock and abandoned mining installations.

The ship sank lower. A jumble of ceramic and metal hemispheres came into view. Beyond them, a range of mountains loomed ghostly gray, lit by Earth-shine. In the absence of any atmosphere, the horizon looked close enough to touch.

Srndhi flipped a switch and the artificial gravity died. Aton felt himself rise up slightly in his seat. The ship settled into one of a series of concrete landing bays, and there was a distant vibration, then the jolt of final contact. Srndhi moved levers, and the ship powered down.

"Are you in telepathic range with the ambassador now?" Aton asked as Srndhi left its stool and bustled around the control room, stowing items and shutting down systems.

"No. Regrettably not."

"What about Malice? Can you sense her presence at all?"

Srndhi paused for a long moment. "It is hard. There are so many Human Selves nearby. But I think not." The Xest picked up some documents that Aton recognized as the diplomatic papers it had salvaged from the King's palace on Minion. Then it located its offspring and placed it on the control panel. "The small self retains custody of the ship. We are ready to exit?"

"Maybe we better wait for them to enter." There were scraping metallic sounds outside the ship as umbilicals locked on. The airlock cycled, then slid open. A sanitation unit rolled in venting mist from its nozzles.

"Harmful to Xest respiration?" Srndhi asked nervously.

"No. Just to viruses and bacteria."

An immigration robot followed. It was an old humanoid design, its pseudoflesh crusty and peeling. "I need your names, origins, and cargo," it stated flatly.

Srndhi was deaf to all sound and unable to pick up thoughts from an artificial intelligence, so Aton acted as intermediary. The process took less than a minute.

"Obey the laws," the robot told them. "No coercion of any kind. No confiscation of private property or damage to same. Lock your ship when you leave, and don't expect any handouts. Welcome to Luna." It turned and rolled away.

"That's all?" Aton shook his head. "Almost any other place I've been, there were more formalities than that."

"Libertarian principles of nongovernment," Srndhi said. "Evidently, they still apply, in which case our mission may be even more difficult than one feared. Still, we must try."

Together, they left the ship.

CHAPTER 10 _____

The access tunnel was a pressurized flexible tube linking the ship's airlock with the main dome on Luna. It smelled of disinfectant and unwashed human flesh, and its floor plates were dark with dirt.

The Xest hesitated in front of a pair of doors at the end. "So many Human Selves ahead of us," it said. "And much disorder. Much distress."

"It's the main recreation dome, according to the map," said Aton. "But whatever it is, we'll find our way through to the administrative sector as quickly as we can." He pushed the doors open.

He found himself in a huge arena, like an exhibition hall, under an immense hemisphere of tarnished steel. The space was cluttered with little ramshackle structures, storefronts and houses bolted together from metal panels, like a high-technology refugee camp. Low lunar gravity enabled the shacks to be stacked on top of one another in tottering pyramids six and seven stories high. Music was blaring; babies were screaming; people were shouting. The place stank of humanity.

A beggar whose legs had been amputated at the

knee came crawling across the metal floor, dragging himself forward with deformed, callused hands. "Need a guide, friend?" He gave Aton a toothless grin. His face was mottled with radiation scars, and one of his eyes was opaque with cataracts. "I been around. I show you whatever you want."

"No thanks." Aton sidestepped past him.

"Spare a couple dollars, then. I can't get no work. Mining accident. Friend?" His voice receded plaintively behind them.

"Well, hi there." A young black man in a silver jump suit and heavy gold jewelry stepped into Aton's path. He grinned. "Is you looking? Hey, I got synthetics from Cygnus—the *real* machine, give a *permanent* high, know it? Or Senstim? Or sex?" He gestured, and an animated holo image appeared in front of them: a naked twelve-year-old girl sucking her thumb and fingering herself obscenely. She pirouetted, flaunting perfect flesh in full color. "Or if you go the other way—" A young boy took her place, fondling himself and leering. "All legal, all human, no coercion, so come on, now. It don't cost but a few dollars."

"No." Aton said it as decisively as he could.

The pimp shrugged. The holos flicked out of existence and he sauntered away.

Others quickly took his place, wheedling, demanding, making offers. They ignored Srndhi and surrounded Aton, and although no one actually touched him, the effect was threatening. He pushed past a mutant with an extra pair of vestigial, stumpy legs sprouting from his hips; he turned away from a five-year-old girl whose face was half eaten by cancer; he stepped around a creaking, rusty robot carrying an emaciated cripple in its arms. "Good luck," the cripple called faintly, holding out a begging bowl and searching for him with blind eyes. "I can bring you good luck."

"Let's cut through here," Aton said to Srndhi. He started along an alley that bisected the heaped mass of ramshackle buildings. "According to the map, we have to get across to the other side of this dome."

"I will follow." The alien shuddered. "But one finds it most painful."

Aton strode past food vendors peddling synthetic steak, storefront drug parlors, sensie theaters, and flesh shows. The crowd of beggars and hustlers gradually fell behind, and he noticed a gradual change in the people around him. A few were still dressed in rags, but others had customized faces and rebuilt bodies fitted out in shiny plastic fabrics and exotic furs.

"The decadent rich," Aton commented. "Out for some cheap thrills in the raunchy part of town."

A half-naked, beautiful woman came wandering over, studying him with frank physical interest. She tossed a cascade of blond curls aside and smiled, exposing perfect teeth.

Aton stared at her. She was wearing nothing but kneelength boots and a black plastic T-shirt. Its low neck was stretched tight around her plump breasts, and its hem reached only to her hips, leaving her crotch and thighs completely naked.

She eyed his clothes. He was still in the peasant

outfit that Malice had given him on Minion. Since escaping from the King's prison, there had been no opportunity to change into anything else. "Hey, country boy," she said, and laughed.

"Sorry," Aton told her. "Not interested."

She reached for a concealed zipper and opened the T-shirt down the front, exposing the entire length of her body to him. "No?" She cupped her hands under her big breasts, and lifted them. She moved forward till her nipples were almost touching his chest.

Aton found himself staring at her body. He made himself look up at her face. "Some other time. We have to get to the administrative sector."

She closed the zipper and shrugged. "Okay, honey." Her tone of voice changed from seductive to matter-of-fact. "Wanna know where it is?"

"We have a map."

"Let me see that." She took it out of his hand. "No, this is way out of date. Hell, I may as well show you. You, and your—your friend, there, whatever he is."

"How much will it cost us?"

She gave him a look of injured pride. "Now that's an insult, country boy."

"Everyone here seems to be operating some sort of scam. Why should you be any different?"

She put her arm around his waist and started walking with him, letting her half-naked body rub against his. "If you was less of a country boy, you could tell. I'm from one of the other domes. Just here looking for some fun." She felt the muscles of his arm and smiled. "Hey, I like that. What's your name? I'm

Lorraine." Her arm slipped down, and her hand moved around, feeling between his legs. "You *sure* you ain't interested?"

Her physical presence was intoxicating, like an adolescent fantasy. But Aton pushed her hand away. "My friend"—he gestured to Srndhi—"is suffering. We have to get to the administrative sector."

She rolled her eyes. "You are no fun at *all*." She sighed. "All right, then. This way." She stopped trying to touch him and led him briskly toward the far side of the dome.

Aton checked that Srndhi was still beside him, and followed. They emerged from the clutter of buildings and moved around the perimeter to an exit. "You go through here"—the woman gestured—"down ten levels, across the green ramp, up a level—" She paused. "It's kind of complicated."

"Srndhi," said Aton. "Can you see it in her mind?"

"One has difficulties. One cannot. Perhaps because, so many minds. I'm sorry."

Aton turned back to Lorraine. "Maybe you could write it down?"

She laughed merrily. "Honey, there ain't no one on Luna knows how to *write*. I guess I'll have to show you. You just have to promise me one thing."

"What's that?"

"A kiss."

"That's all?"

"That's all." She winked at him. "Unless you decide you want something more."

She led them through ancient corridors hewn out of lunar rock, along motorpaths that had seized up and were silted with grime, and into an underground atrium with sunlamps beaming down onto limp vegetation in artificial soil.

Everywhere they went, there were beggars, cripples, and homeless children sleeping on the floors or holding out their hands. "Why so many?" Srndhi said, looking around, waving its legs in distress. "Can they not see, the health of the individual and the health of the group are the same?"

"Don't worry your head about it," Lorraine told him. "They're just too stupid to stop having kids, that's all. So they die young. It takes care of itself."

"What about crime?" said Aton. "With so much poverty—"

"Crime?" She looked at him as if he was crazy. "You mean, one person taking from another?" She shook her head, making the blond curls bob. "That's coercion, honey." She gestured at one of the many police robots they'd seen, rolling slowly past. "Anyone try anything, the bots take him in."

She led them up some stairs, then along a walkway overlooking the atrium, past a succession of doors. "Up ahead is what you want," she told Aton.

"Can you sense Twnde's consciousness yet?" he asked Srndhi.

"No." The alien was trailing behind, moving listlessly. "One senses only the clamor of Human Selves."

"All right, this is it." The woman stopped and smiled.

"It looks more like a residential zone than—"

"Sure is. But it's as far as I go." She moved closer to him, her lips parted, showing just the tip of her pink tongue. "Now, about that kiss." She linked her hands behind his neck, and pressed her body against him. He felt the mass of her breasts pushing against him like a fat cushion, and her lips against his, soft but insistent. Her tongue probed into his mouth.

He pulled sharply away. There was something—wrong. The taste of her was alien and strange.

He reexamined her face. It didn't just have the perfection of plastic surgery. It was synthetic. "You're not human," he stammered.

She pouted at him. "You don't have to get all worked up about it." She tilted her head to one side. "So you've never done it with a Sim? I didn't think you had. Think about it: a girl who never gets tired, who's always in the mood, with some special talents you never even dreamed of."

Aton felt suddenly dizzy. The strange taste was still in his mouth. "What do you want from me? What is this?"

"Hey, take it easy." She stroked his arm, watching his face closely. "Come on. You come along with me."

He tried to resist; then he stumbled forward as if he was no longer in proper control of his body. She turned and pressed her palm against the nearest door, and it slid open.

"This'll take awhile," she said over her shoulder to Srndhi. "You hang around if you want. Ain't no harm going to come to him. It's his own free will, know what I mean?" She turned and nudged Aton into the room. "And he'll get value for money. You can be sure of that."

"No!" Srndhi's voice reached Aton faintly, as if from a different level of reality. "Aton, what is this ritual? Your thoughts are—"

The rest was cut off as she closed the door.

Aton found himself in a tiny room almost filled by a huge bed. All the furnishings were pink. The ceiling was mirrored, and it was low, just inches above his head.

"I don't understand," he said thickly. He steadied himself with his hand against the wall.

"Seduced by a kiss, honey." She laughed happily. Her fingers quickly loosened his pants.

Aton realized he was intensely aroused. But it felt as if his body belonged to someone else. "My muscles," he blurted, hearing himself slurring the words. "Can't—"

She gave him a push and he fell onto the bed. "It's okay, you don't have to do nothing." She licked her lips. "Just leave it to the expert."

The next hour was blurred, a waking dream of wet sex and warm flesh, his body lying inert yet electrified. She tantalized him, pulled away, then engulfed him with herself. Her smell was an aphrodisiac; her grip on him was relentless. For a while he drifted, hallucinating Malice's face staring down at him. He tried to reach for her, but his muscles disobeyed him. Then Lorraine's large, soft breasts pressed against his face and he found himself back in the little room, the bed bouncing under him, her body slapping against his as she brought him to an aching, gasping climax.

Minutes or hours later, she was gone, and he found himself lying cold and naked, his genitals slightly sore and his flesh covered in goose bumps. He realized, with distant surprise, that he was able to move. He sat up, blinking.

His clothes were stacked on a tiny chair beside the bed. He grabbed them, and felt in his pocket for the box of gold wafers that Srndhi had given him. The box was gone; in its place, he found a 3-D color-card. The warmth of his hand activated it. "Hi, country boy." The voice was faint but distinct, and Lorraine's image winked at him. "Give me a call: 323-187-098. Anytime." For a tantalizing moment, her clothes disappeared, revealing her naked body. Then the card recycled. "Hi, country boy—"

Aton swore. He thrust it back in his pocket, pulled on his clothes, and slid the door open.

Outside in the corridor he found a yellow form slumped on the floor in a tangle of legs. "Srndhi!" he called.

The Xest moved slowly to its feet. "One could not open the door from outside to offer help." The synthesized voice was sluggish and dull. "One waited."

"How long was I in there?"

"Time is hard to measure here, and one is no longer in range of one's small self, in the ship. Two hours, perhaps."

"Srndhi, I'm sorry. By the time I realized what she was, it was too late. Her mouth contained some sort of drug. I couldn't move properly. The money's gone and—"

"It does not matter. There is no blame. While you were in there, a police robot passed by."

Aton paused, absorbing this fact. "So why didn't you ask for help? If there's any law here at all—"

"I did request help. The robot stated that yours was a commercial transaction by free consent."

"That's not true. I was drugged."

"I had deduced this, and informed the robot. It told me that such aphrodisiacs are common and legal. It is the individual's responsibility to protect himself. You pressed lips of your free will."

"Bastards." Aton experienced a spasm of rage, imagining himself grabbing the woman by the neck, shaking her, squeezing his thumbs on her throat—

"Please." Srndhi sounded pained. "That will not restore our money, and in any case she is merely a machine. Come, I now know where to find Twnde."

Aton blinked. "You do?"

"One inquired of the police robot. It responded." The Xest started along the corridor. "You will follow?"

"Of course." Aton went after it. "But you sound so full of despair."

"This is a place of unhappiness." Srndhi led the way into an elevator and pressed a number with one of its legs. The doors slid shut and the car moved upward.

They emerged into a lobby whose roof was armorglass. Overhead, the sky was black, sprinkled with stars. Planet Earth hung in the darkness, blue seas streaked with silvery cloud.

The lobby was deserted except for a cleaning robot, grinding slowly to and fro. "Now one senses the consciousness of Twnde-Xest." Srndhi's legs stiffened, and it walked faster. "This way, Aton." It led him through an archway decorated with peeling pictures of alien worlds and ancient human space vehicles. At the top of the arch was the Federation crest, in faded gold.

They traversed a long, deserted corridor. "Where is everyone?" Aton asked. "Is it a sleep period?"

"Perhaps. One senses few human minds here." The alien stopped suddenly. "Oh."

"What is it?"

There was a long pause. "It's Twnde. Worse than I feared. There is a Xest condition one finds hard to describe, a sickness. The 'eating sickness.' "

"What do you mean?"

"You will see soon enough." Srndhi started moving again, more urgently than before.

Aton hurried to keep up. "But he's alive? Can he help us?"

"We shall have to give help before we can receive it. We will need your courage, Aton. Quickly; this way."

chapter xi _____

He was being tossed from side to side, and someone was crying out in a voice pitched high with fear. Aton woke and groped behind him for the dagger. His fingers closed around its hilt. This time there was no Chthonic beast attacking, just the three of them in the boat, but the boat was rocking wildly, water was slopping in, the tunnel was moving past impossibly fast, and there was a roaring noise, growing louder.

"I fell asleep," Gwinnie was shouting. "What's happening? Why's the water coming over the sides?"

Aton sat up. His body moved sluggishly, as if a great weight were pressing on him. He discovered that the boat was lying much deeper than before, and the river had become a ferocious torrent. They were careening along, spinning as they went.

"Higher gravity," Aton muttered.

"What?" Oris was still groggy with sleep. She looked around in confusion.

"In the apetiles' cave, it was lower. Here, it's higher. Feel it pulling us down?" To himself, he added: *everything is inverted.*

"It sounds like a waterfall up ahead," Gwinnie called over her shoulder. "Oh god, I can't even swim!"

Aton got up onto his knees and glanced either side. The banks of the river were sheer rock, worn smooth by the torrent. The tunnel was closing in, narrowing to a tube just ten feet across. "We have to get out."

There was a grinding, rasping noise, and the boat rocked violently. Waves splashed in, ice-cold. The boat lurched, scraped across more underwater rocks, and a gash suddenly appeared in the bottom. Water squirted in, quickly pooling around Aton's feet.

He saw a ledge in the rockface to his left. He dropped the dagger, grabbed Gwinnie by her hips, and thrust her upward. "Grab that ledge," he told her.

Her fingers scrabbled for a hold. She cried in pain as sharp stone tore her flesh. Then she managed to get a grip, and held on.

"Gwinnie!" Oris was shouting. "Help me!" She reached out to the girl.

"I can't," Gwinnie cried.

"Damn you!" Oris seized the hem of Aton's tunic instead, as the boat sank under her. Aton maintained his grip on Gwinnie, and the boat was swept away, half submerged, disappearing into the darkness.

The torrent of water engulfed Aton up to his chest, surging against him. He kept one hand on Gwinnie as she dangled with her fingers still keeping a tenuous hold on the ledge. With his other hand, he reached for the rock himself. The water was roaring all around them, and gravity was tearing at his muscles.

He curled his fingers into a fissure and dragged

himself up. He saw Oris doing the same. As his legs came out of the water his body seemed to grow leaden, but the water was no longer trying to pull him away.

Aton climbed up onto the ledge. He reached down, then, and grabbed one of Gwinnie's wrists, just as her fingers were finally losing their grip and she was moaning in fear at being claimed by the water. He lifted her up onto the ledge beside him, then turned to check that Oris, also, had climbed to safety.

The three of them lay there for a moment, gasping for breath, shivering with cold and shock. There was hardly any lichen growing in this part of the tunnel, and it was very dark. "You okay?" Aton called to Gwinnie.

She nodded. Her face was a faint shape in the gloom. "Just my fingers. Bleeding a bit."

"You saved us," he told her.

"I did?"

"You stopped us, by holding on to the rock."

"So now we can die here, instead of in the river," said Oris, her voice mocking him. "Unless you can see some way out that I can't see."

Aton turned and looked back along the tunnel the way they'd come. The ledge they were on was a couple of feet wide, but it narrowed and merged into smooth vertical rock.

He looked in the other direction, further down the river. The ledge continued, but seemed to end abruptly where the tunnel itself ended, in a featureless black hole. "I'll go check," Aton said.

He felt his way forward, looking carefully before

taking each step. The dark water foamed below, ready to claim him if he fell. Up ahead, the roaring noise was deafeningly loud, and spray wafted back into his face on gusts of chill air.

Aton reached the point where the ledge terminated. He got down on his stomach and wriggled forward till he could peer over the edge. Beside him and a little way below, the river gushed out and cascaded down, disappearing into blackness. It seemed to be a vertical shaft twenty feet or more in diameter, pockmarked with the mouths of other tunnels, some of them spewing water like the one Aton was in.

He peered down into the blackness. There was a strong current of air sweeping past him—toward what? Faintly, almost obscured by the torrents of water, he saw a spot of light in the extreme depths below. He blinked, trying to clear his vision. He looked again, and was certain: the spot of light was real.

He inspected the walls of the vertical shaft. They were wet and slick but craggy, crisscrossed with fissures.

There was faint noise from behind him, almost lost in the din of the waterfall. Aton turned his head and strained to listen. It was Gwinnie, shouting something.

He cursed and scrambled away from the precipice. He got up onto his feet and hurried back along the ledge.

The two women were dark, indistinct shapes. Oris was the larger of the two. He saw her move suddenly, her arm jerking forward, and something gleamed briefly. Gwinnie shrieked and clutched herself, backing away.

"Gwinnie!" Aton shouted.

"You want her?" said Oris. She pushed the girl toward him. "Here she is."

Gwinnie tottered forward, clutching her stomach. Dark blood was pulsing out. It splashed against Aton's skin, thick and warm. He caught her under the arms and she hung there, shuddering and making choking noises.

Aton laid her down on the ledge. The girl's eyes rolled up as she lost consciousness. He stared up at Oris in disbelief. "You killed her."

Oris took a step forward. She was holding the dagger that Aton had dropped in the bottom of the boat. She eyed Gwinnie's frail body, then kicked the girl off the ledge into the river. It swept her away in an instant and she was gone, into the darkness of the shaftway where the water cascaded into oblivion.

"Why?" said Aton. He felt his rage rising inside him.

"She refused me. She was no longer mine."

"You're truly insane." He was watching the dagger, alert for any sign that she would come for him next. He stood up and backed away from her. "You killed Votnik too, didn't you?"

Oris stood calmly, watching him. "How do you figure that?"

"Because he never took risks. He wouldn't have gone near that animal. And the wound in his chest that killed him was older than the others, and deeper, as if it had been made with a sharp pointed rock. My guess is you crept over to him while I was asleep, killed him, then dragged him to where I'd laid the snare. You hoped some creature would be lured by the bait, and would take the blame."

"You're quite right," she said calmly.

Aton shook his head. "Was Votnik another one who refused you, and failed you?"

"Yes."

"My god, were you having some sort of sexual relationship with *him*? Was that why he let you get close enough to kill him?"

"Correct."

Aton stood there in the darkness, trying to think, with the water still roaring beside him, and the woman standing watching him, the knife in her hand. "What about Snyder?" he asked suddenly. "Damn it, yes—there was no way his skull could have been crushed like that by natural causes. Back in the apetile cave, I jumped in the river first, with Votnik, then Gwinnie—which left you with Snyder. You clubbed him, threw him in, then jumped in yourself."

"No." Her voice was dispassionate. "I knocked him unconscious and left him there for the apetiles. One of them must have crushed his skull, then thrown him in." She shrugged. "If a tool no longer serves its purpose, you throw it away." She took a step toward him. "You were poisoning all of them, bit by bit. Even Jacko."

Aton edged backward. No more than fifty feet behind him, he knew, was the sheer precipice—the vertical shaft with water pouring down toward the tiny, distant dot of light. "So now there's just the two of us," he said. "Is that what you wanted?"

"That depends." She paused. "What are you going

to do, Aton? Are you going to recognize my authority now, or do I have to kill you too?"

"You'd be crazy to kill me. You said yourself, there's no way to survive alone in Chthon."

"Maybe I am crazy, Aton." She smiled.

He eyed the gap between them, and weighed the possibility of kicking out at her. But she was alert and ready for him. She would easily avoid the kick, grab his ankle, and throw him down into the torrent.

"If we cooperate, we can still get out of here," he told her.

She didn't answer. She took another step closer.

"There's a vertical shaft, back behind me," he went on. "That's where the waterfall is. It's incredibly deep—but there's light at the bottom. White light. Do you realize what that means?"

"No. What does it mean, Aton?" Her voice sounded mechanical and disinterested, but her eyes gleamed in the dimness as she watched his face and his body.

"There's no white light inside Chthon. Only lichen, glowing green. Do you see? We could climb down to it—"

She nodded. "You may be right. I've never doubted that you're a useful man, Aton. But you still have to submit to me."

"Like Gwinnie, you mean? Become your servant?"

"Yes."

"You know I can't do that."

"Bastard!" She leaped at him suddenly. The blade flashed as she swung it at him. He dodged and lost his footing and cried out as he fell on his back on the ledge. One arm flailed into emptiness, but with his free hand he grabbed a crevice in the rock and steadied himself.

He realized he was cut. He didn't feel the pain, but warm wetness was running across his shoulder. His rage pounded inside him, and he realized his rhetoric about cooperation had been meaningless. There was no way the two of them could coexist. He hated her for what she'd done, and he'd kill her if he had the opportunity.

She fell down onto him and he felt her breath on his face, the point of the blade pricking the side of his neck. Her body was an immense weight pinning him. "Submit, Aton," she told him. Her voice was beyond all reason.

chapter xii _____

Aton opened his mouth to speak—then spat in her face. The saliva caught her in the eyes and she jerked her head back, blinking. Her weight still pinned him, but he turned his head and grabbed her wrist in his teeth. He bit hard, feeling tendons bend and click between his jaws. He tasted blood, heard her scream.

She groped for him with her free hand. He seized her hair, wrenched her head back, then slammed it into the rocky wall beside them.

She tried to grab his genitals but seemed dizzy and uncoordinated. He released her wrist, pulled his leg up, and kicked her off him. She fell off the ledge, and her legs splashed into the river, but he still kept his grip on her hair. She dangled in his grip, flailing wildly.

He seized her wrist and smacked it against the sharp edge of the ledge. He did it again, and again, till the knife came out of her hand.

He paused, then, and tried to calm his racing pulse. She reached up and tried to grab his wrist, where he was still holding her by the hair, but he picked up the knife and stabbed her hand with it. "Lie still!" he shouted at her.

She yelled in pain and fury, but she was helpless, suspended in the torrent of water.

Slowly, grunting with the effort, Aton stood up, pulling her out of the water by her hair. He kicked her body to turn it, and dumped her facedown on the ledge. He grabbed the wrist he had bitten and broken against the rock, and found it slick with blood. He forced it up behind her back, till she screamed. He maintained the pressure, pinning her there.

Slowly, he knelt down, then sat on her buttocks. He shook his head to clear it.

"Kill me," she shouted at him, her cheek pressed against wet stone. "Kill me now. I'd rather die than—"

"Shut up!" he yelled at her. He forced her wrist further up behind her back, threatening to dislocate her shoulder.

He used the knife to slice through her convict tunic. Methodically, he cut it into two long strips. She swore at him, and tried to throw him off her back, but he held her down, the high gravity making it impossible for her to dislodge him.

He tied one end of the cloth around her wounded wrist, then seized her other wrist, and lashed them together. He grabbed her ankle; she kicked wildly, but he looped the cloth around it, and held it. Within a couple of minutes both her ankles were tied, and he rolled her over onto her back.

She reared up, trying to butt him with her head. He kicked her in the chest, forcing her back down onto the rocky ledge, then sat on her belly. "Remember when you had me like this, tied with my hands behind me?" he said. He paused, breathing heavily. "Remember the things you did?"

She swallowed hard and said nothing. Her nostrils flared; her eyes were wild. She clenched her jaw and jerked her body from side to side, trying to free herself.

She was naked underneath him, now that he had cut her clothes off her, and she was helpless. He ran his hand over her skin, feeling the muscles rippling in spasms beneath it. He stroked his fingers across her breasts, then grabbed her flesh brutally, watching her twist and flinch. "You hurt me, didn't you?" he shouted at her, his grip tightening. He raised the knife in his other hand. "The first thing you did was gouge my chest, with the ax you stole from me." He touched the tip of the blade to her skin between her breasts. "Let's see how you enjoy that." He pressed down, and saw a small dark bead of blood well up.

He paused for a long moment. There was no sound other than the roaring of the river, the pounding of blood in his ears.

Suddenly Aton pulled back. He threw the knife aside. It pinwheeled away and splashed into the rushing water. "Gwinnie was right," he said. The anger was gone from his voice. He sounded weary and disgusted. "There's been too much death, too much violence." He glared at Oris. "Once I could have done it. I could have done all the things to you that you did to me, and more." He looked at his own hands, then at her naked body. "I would have tortured you and raped you, without hesitation or regret."

She said nothing, watching him and waiting to see what he was going to do.

"But if I inflict the same things on you that you did to me, that means I'm no better than you are."

She gave him a slow, crazy smile. "So you're as weak as the rest of them, after all." She lurched up and twisted, throwing him off her. Aton was caught by surprise. He lost his balance and fell to one side.

She brought her knees up. Even with her ankles tied, she was able to kick out at him. Her heels caught him in the stomach.

Aton felt himself falling. He reached for something to save himself—and caught hold of her leg. Lying on her back with her hands tied behind her, she had no way to grab the rocks and stop herself from sliding. As he fell off the ledge, he dragged her after him. Together, they splashed into the torrent.

The water closed around him. He struggled up to the surface and found her face a few feet away, half submerged, eyeing him in triumph. "You've killed us both!" he shouted at her.

Then Aton felt himself tumbling out and down, falling with the water into emptiness. He saw Oris falling above him, her body turning amid the spray. Wind roared in his ears. He looked down into the black void, and his throat went tight with fear. There was nothing to catch hold of, no way to stop himself plummeting. He heard himself screaming as he fell, and the scream echoed in the shaftway.

Seconds passed. He fell faster, and the air tore at his clothes and lashed his hair into his eyes. He felt something nudge his body and saw it was Oris. Her slightly smaller frame offered less resistance to the air; she was falling faster, overtaking him. Her eyes were clenched tight shut, and her knees were pulled up to her breasts. Wrists and ankles still tied, she went past him, tumbling as she fell.

The tiny white point at the bottom of the shaft was growing larger. It was lost from view for a moment as Aton fell through a new torrent of water spewing from another hole in the side of the shaftway. Then the white light reappeared, a circle now, growing bigger and still bigger.

Oris was a diminishing black speck below him. Aton fell after her, toward the whiteness, and it glared like the open door of a furnace.

The walls of the shaft were a blur, and he realized that if he veered toward them, they would rip him apart. He tried to balance himself in the center of the shaft as the air pressed fiercely up against him.

Then the shaftway opened out either side of him, and he was falling into the whiteness itself.

He stared around in confusion. He was—outside. He looked back and saw the shaftway receding from him, a hole in what now looked like a dark, featureless, stony plain. But the plain was curved. As Aton spun out into the white void, he saw more of the surface below. It was a sphere; a featureless black planet, pierced by the shaftway along one axis.

He had emerged from Chthon.

Internode _____

The black planet slowly receded from him. He was isolated in the whiteness—white space, studded with black pinpricks that were stars.

His chest ached with the need to breathe. Yet somehow breathing was not necessary. He opened his mouth to shout; but he could not speak. He spun like a slow-motion ballet dancer, paralyzed and stranded in the void.

"Reborn," said a voice.

It came from inside him, and was the same as the voice he had imagined when he had drifted into sleep, in the boat in the river.

"You have paid. Now you are free."

"What? Who—"

"Remember, your past life." All his lost memories came pouring back into his mind: an avalanche of color and sound. "You were imprisoned, once, as incurable. Condemned, by your genes."

Aton remembered, now, his banishment. He had been shut away in the garnet mines of Chthon. He had schemed to escape, had sacrificed friends and enemies alike to serve his purpose on the hard trek. He *had* escaped, and had encountered Bedeker, the man who had escaped before him.

Other memories crowded in. He and Bedeker had formed an uneasy alliance, had uncovered Aton's true ancestry, and finally Aton had confronted Malice and killed her, unable to cope with his own self-loathing.

He had been exiled back to Chthon—and this time, he'd gone voluntarily, in a pact with Bedeker. For it turned out that Bedeker had been a tool of Chthon. Chthon was more than a planet, it was a mineral entity—a sentient being whose telepathic intelligence resided in its molten core. It accepted those who were evil, and abused them, for it was itself a malignant thing that detested all biological life.

Aton had settled in the caves of Chthon like a damned soul, dwelling with a woman named Coquina, and they had had a son. But gradually it became apparent that Chthon was not content merely to harbor and torment the people who were condemned to subsist in it. It made contact with other nonbiological entities—mineral beings from another galaxy. Together with them, it planned to annihilate all human life in a cataclysmic metaphysical explosion: *Phthor.*

Aton and his son—and others whose faces now flashed briefly before him—fought to avert the destruction. They failed: the explosion occurred. But it was contained: Chthon was vaporized, as were all those in it, while the rest of the galaxy survived unharmed.

"But I was in Chthon at the moment of devastation," Aton stated in his mind. "There was no way out. I must have been killed."

"Yes, and no. The cataclysm was sufficiently violent to collapse the structure of matter. You became the center of what is known as a singularity. A black hole. In it, all laws of the physical universe were suspended. All probabilities became equal. From your last thoughts, a pseudoreality was created, outside of spacetime."

"And that's where I am now?"

"That is where you have been. You inflicted on yourself a compensation for your past crimes. Where once you manipulated, tortured, and killed other people, now you placed yourself at their mercy. You learned to endure their cruelty. And finally, you learned to rise above the concept of primitive revenge."

"Everything else was inverted also," Aton realized. "The temperature; and time, because I grew younger while I was there; and even the structure of the planet. The way up, to the surface, was down—"

"Gravity was a repulsive force," the voice told him. "Stronger at the surface, repelling you from the planet, into nonspace."

"But if this is just a dream—"

"No. It is a reality, built from the surviving incarnation of your consciousness."

"Then who are you?" Aton asked suddenly. "Are you just an extension of my own thoughts?"

"We are the extragalactic mineral entities, who once collaborated with Chthon. We were deceived by it, into the belief that biological life is an abomination.

We see now that it is not so. We presented you with the image of Bedeker, to tell you where you were when you reawoke in the inverted world created from your own consciousness. Then we monitored your progress. We saw how it was possible for you to redeem yourself. We wish, now, to undo the damage we once did—the vast explosion which killed thousands of innocent humans and other life forms."

"But it happened," Aton answered. "I remember the last moments. It was uncontrollable."

"From a singularity, there are worm holes through spacetime," the voice told him. "Some lead backward."

"You mean, I could emerge back *before* the catastrophe, and try to avert it?"

"There is only one universe. But at every instant, we make choices that determine its future, and our own. There was one crucial choice in your life: where you first found the Minionette, Malice, and she confessed that she was your mother. You turned away from her, and from then on you were lost. Had you managed to accept her, and yourself, everything would have evolved differently."

Aton thought back. "Yes, I remember—a room in a spotel. She told me the truth, and I fled. But the dream-memories I've been having conflict with that. In those dream-memories, I *didn't* run away from her. We went to Minion together. I was discontent, but still, I was following her."

"Those dream-memories were of the alternate life you could have led," the voice told him. "They were not real."

"You put them in my head?"

"We transferred them from an alternate reality to show you what awaits you if you take that other branch through fourspace. You can enter that reality now, if you choose, back at the time when you found her, after searching for her for four years."

He thought carefully. There had to be a price to pay. "What must I do for you in return, to be granted this second chance?"

"You must destroy Chthon. Not this dead world that you constructed from your own mind; the Chthon in realspace, an evil mineral entity that attempted— will attempt—to end all life in your universe. You must destroy it in such a way that no lives are lost. We collaborated with Chthon; but we were wrong. We must undo that wrong. But *we* cannot move backward in time, and we are impossibly distant in space. The work must be done by you."

Aton remembered the most recent of his dream-memories. "It seems that it might be possible. I had reached the moon; I might be able to do what you ask."

"If you accept our bargain, your consciousness will be projected back into your former self. You will find yourself aged twenty-five, confronted with the Minionette in the spotel. You will remember nothing of our conversation, or of your possible future." The voice sounded enigmatic, yet severe: a stern, impersonal warning.

"But if I will remember nothing, how will I know that I have to destroy Chthon to fulfill our bargain?"

"You will not know explicitly. But your timeline will link with Chthon. And you will feel an obligation."

"And if I decide, now, not to accept your bargain?"

"With regret, we will break contact. It cannot be sustained indefinitely. The singularity is unstable. It is accreting matter. The suspension of normal physical laws works both ways: that which can be created can also be destroyed. It is impossible to predict what will happen. Most likely, your consciousness will fragment. We do not know."

The choice was no choice at all. "Very well," said Aton. "I accept."

"Good. Prepare yourself for a discontinuity—"

"Wait! What about Oris? Was she real? Is she—"

"Everything here is real. We cannot predict—"

There was a blinding, silent flash.

"I am more than your lover," the beautiful red-haired woman was telling him. "Aton? Are you listening?"

He was momentarily distracted by his image in the mirror above the cleansing facility in the little room of the spotel. For some reason, his reflection seemed impossibly young. Yet at the same time, it was completely familiar; his everyday self, aged twenty-five. "I'm sorry," he told her. He shook his head, as if haunted by afterimages of some other time and place. "Maybe it's the effect of all the FTL flights I've been taking. Go on."

She took his hand. "Aton. On my world, there are customs that are unacceptable elsewhere. The women are genetically modified. They live for two centuries or more, and show few signs of age." She drew a deep breath. "As their first husband grows old, they remarry—the son."

He frowned. He had come here to fulfill his romantic yearning for her, not to listen to a summary of her cultural history. "Why are you telling me this?"

"Your father visited my world. We became involved. I became pregnant and you—are my son."

He jerked his hand out of her grasp and retreated from her across the room.

"Stop!" she called to him. "Please, Aton."

"You expect me to stay with you?" He stared at her incredulously.

She ran to him. "At least wait a few days before you decide. Let me show you my world; it's your world, too, remember that. A few days, at least, Aton."

He took a step back, toward the door. "No." He sensed that what she had revealed to him was true. It resonated within him, and it was intolerable.

Then a new thought came to him, of the future he would experience if he left now, eliminating her from his life. He imagined emptiness punctuated by moments of uncontrollable rage, as he inflicted his loneliness and self-loathing upon anyone who attempted to win his trust or love.

He looked at her again. She was staring at him with total devotion. Mother, and lover. Impossible; yet if he rejected her, he sensed he was doomed.

And if he stayed with her? He couldn't imagine it.

"You want to show me your world," he repeated, his tongue forming the words awkwardly.

She nodded. "We can go now. My transit capsule

is outside; within a day, we can be on Minion. It's a different language, but I have a biochip that will enable you to speak it. There's so much you have to learn; so much I can teach you, if you'll come with me."

He kept his distance from her, as if afraid of touching her. Awkwardly, he nodded his assent.

CHAPTER 11 _____

The metal door was scratched and dented, as if it had endured centuries of use. A tarnished nameplate was set in its center, embossed with alien script. Below it, the translation: FIRST EARTH EMBASSY OF THE COMMUNITY OF XEST.

Aton pushed the door open, revealing a small room illuminated by a single flickering ceiling panel. There were two chairs, both of them broken and repaired with packing tape. A reception desk stood in the center of the room, its surface gray with dust. The place looked as if it had lain empty for years.

"Please follow." Srndhi walked across faded carpet to a connecting door. It raised a leg, pushed the door open, and stopped.

The room beyond was completely filled with a huge tangled mass of yellow Xest limbs, covering the floor and heaped up against the walls. Buried at the center was the body of Ambassador Twnde itself: a great bloated bladder, legs sprouting from all sides.

Srndhi moved forward and touched one of the limbs with its own. There was a long moment of silence.

"Twnde apologizes for not speaking to you," Srndhi said to Aton, finally. "Its translation device is no longer functioning. I informed it of your help to oneself, and your resourcefulness. It is grateful to you, and says that its pain is eased somewhat by knowing that there is some accord, at least, between our species."

"But what's happened here?"

"One moment." Srndhi went back to the ante-room, and there was the sound of drawers being opened and closed. It returned holding a small metal box. "Twnde asks that I offer it the taphid. It is an honor for me. Please, step back."

Aton recoiled. "Turlingian aphids?"

"There is no danger." Srndhi opened the box. Mist coiled out of it; the contents were frozen near absolute zero.

"What do you mean, no danger? They'll eat through steel, through rock—"

"Please." Srndhi laid the open box on the floor. "Do not be alarmed."

Ambassador Twnde placed the tip of one of its legs in the steaming compartment. Beneath the mist, something pink began to stir and twitch.

"They'll eat him alive," Aton protested.

"Dissolution, yes. Twnde appreciates your concern for its health. It regrets that you should see it in such a humiliating condition. It bids you farewell."

The contents of the metal box were rapidly reaching room temperature. Aton saw fat, pink slugs wriggling out, crawling onto the tip of the Xest's leg and devouring it.

Aton gestured helplessly. "Isn't there a cure for this sickness, whatever it is?"

"Twnde has transferred its knowledge to my self. The cells remember. There is no further need for its physical being. It is an embarrassment."

The leg was visibly shorter, now. The giant Xest stirred restlessly, as if in pain.

"But when the taphids finish with him, they'll start on the room, and everything else."

"The Xest body secretes substances which are poisonous to the taphids. They consume it, but are in turn consumed by it. It is a mutual annihilation." Srndhi turned and started toward the exit. "We should leave Twnde to the contemplation of the void that awaits. It is a sacred moment. Come."

Aton took a last look at the great bulk, its many legs kinked and coiled, sprawling across the floor. He turned and walked out.

"This is a very grave matter," Srndhi said. "Without the ambassador's help, our mission would appear impossible. One can only suggest we should return to the ship, and evaluate our options with its aid."

"All right," Aton agreed. Together, they started back along the corridor, past the long, silent rows of doors. "But explain the eating sickness."

"An analogy will help. One has heard that a desperate human, experiencing chronic thirst, will drink salt water, even though this depletes fluids from the body, worsens the thirst, and leads to further drinking of salt water, in a vicious cycle."

"That's correct," said Aton.

"Certain types of stress and despair can cause a

Xest to behave similarly. It eats its own body, even though this causes it to regenerate—and, even worse, grow additional limbs—so that it becomes larger than it was before. It eats more of itself—and again grows larger. The sense of shame and debt that this incurs merely adds to the hunger."

"And this happened to Twnde because of being isolated here on the moon?"

"Because of that, and because the efforts to promote understanding between the species were a failure. Twnde would have used the taphids itself, except that it had become too large to leave its room, and could not reach the desk containing the sacred box."

They traveled down several levels in an elevator and emerged in a corridor that Aton thought he recognized from before. But as he and Srndhi walked along it, he realized they were in a different part of the lunar complex.

"You have the map?" Srndhi asked.

Aton reached in his pocket, and cursed. "I must have left it in the room where that woman-robot took me."

"Unfortunate. I think we are lost."

Aton groaned. He stopped and looked back, wondering if they should retrace their steps. He looked ahead and saw that the corridor divided. "I can hear voices. Perhaps there'll be another law-enforcement robot that can give directions."

"Perhaps." Srndhi's voice sounded doubtful.

They turned the corner and found themselves entering a large, low-ceilinged room. The place stank of stale sweat and urine. Beggars, mutants, and cripples were sitting and lying on the floor, supervised by strategically positioned robot guards.

A thin, acne-faced man holding a clipboard walked over to Aton and eyed him with professional disinterest. "Help you?"

Aton grimaced at the smell. "All we want—"

"I can't use anything off the alien," the man interrupted, "but I can give you a good price. What are you selling?"

"Selling?"

The man tapped a stylus impatiently on his clipboard. "What are you, from a backwater planet? This is organ trading."

Aton looked again at the wretched figures littering the room. Many lacked hands; some were legless; others had lost their eyes. "These people are waiting for transplants?"

"No, they're *selling*. We get a lot of repeat business. You want an appointment for an evaluation?"

Aton took another look at the human waste strewn across the room, then glared at the petty official in front of him. "This is your filthy little business, is it?"

The man pointed the tip of his stylus at him. "Watch your language, peasant."

Frustration turned to anger. Aton grabbed the man by his collar and shook him. "Watch *my* language?"

The man's eyes widened in surprise. He dropped his clipboard and pried with his fingernails at Aton's wrist.

Aton pushed the man, and he stumbled backward. His head hit the wall and he clutched it, staring at Aton in astonishment. "Guard!" he shouted.

One of the robots was already rolling toward them. It seized Aton under the arms and hoisted him off the floor.

"Mudsucker," the weasel-faced man shouted at Aton. "Where the hell you think you are?"

Aton tried to kick the steel figure holding him. His legs waved ineffectually. The robot started out of the room, taking him with it. "You are under arrest," it droned.

"You will please let him go," said Srndhi. The Xest was standing squarely in front of the exit, leaving no room for the robot to pass.

The robot rolled to a halt. "Obstructing an officer in the course of its duty is an offense," it stated.

"He is guilty of no crime. You will please release him." The alien moved forward determinedly and started tugging at one of the robot's arms.

"Interference with an officer is an offense. You are under arrest also." Another robot came over, stooped, and lifted Srndhi. Together, he and Aton were carried away.

The process was entirely automated. Robots stripped Aton, searched him, sprayed him with disinfectant, then returned his clothes. They processed him like a component on an assembly line, and placed him in a little steel-walled room whose only features were a ventilation grille, a glow panel, a video scanner, and a toilet.

He sat alone on the floor, leaning against the wall, trying to guess what sort of justice he could expect from a system that routinely allowed its citizens to degenerate to the point where they had to sell pieces of their own bodies to avoid starving to death. He wondered too what had happened to Srndhi. The Xest hadn't even tried to resist when it was carried away. It had slumped in the robot's steel arms with its eight legs dangling, and had said nothing.

There was a click from the grille in the ceiling. "You have been charged with assault," a mechanical voice told Aton. "The plaintiff wishes to negotiate. He requests five hundred new dollars in gold, or a donation of body organs of equivalent commercial value. I am authorized to arbitrate in this matter. Please state your response."

Aton stood up. He flexed his muscles, then jumped and kicked out at the opposite wall. His heel crashed into the steel plating, leaving a barely visible dent.

He sat down again. "I have no response."

The grille clicked again and went dead.

A few minutes later, the door of the room opened. Aton stood up quickly, ready to try to defend himself. He found one of the police robots outside, accompanied by a sharp-featured woman in a black jump suit. She was petite and had short-cropped black hair, and moved with an air of authority. "You in charge of the alien?" she asked without any preliminaries.

Aton evaluated her. Her eyes were alert and she had an intelligent face. She stood with her hands on her hips, as if she was impatient for him to answer. "I'm not in charge of anyone," he told her.

"But you're traveling together. You and the Xest."

"Yes, that's correct."

"The alien won't say anything. I'll get the charges against you dropped if you'll get him to talk."

Aton thought for a moment. "Whether the alien chooses to talk is none of my business," he told her cautiously. "But I'm willing to try to mediate, depending on what you want."

She beckoned. "Come with me."

Aton followed her along a narrow corridor, the police robot rolling close behind him.

"What were you looking for down on level seventeen, anyway?" She glanced at Aton over her shoulder.

"We were looking for the exit."

"Interesting." She thumbed a sensor plate beside a door, and it opened. "Your friend's in here. Do you have business on Luna, or what?"

Aton looked through the doorway. The small cell was identical to the one he had been in. Srndhi was slumped on the floor in the corner. "My Xest companion is here on . . . diplomatic business," said Aton.

"Is he okay?"

The Xest slowly lifted itself up onto its legs and walked across to Aton, saying nothing.

"Xests find this kind of human environment stressful," Aton said. "But I don't think there's anything physically wrong."

The woman paused thoughtfully. "You two should come with me. We can forget the assault and obstruction charges. There's some things I want to know."

CHAPTER 12 _____

They rode up with her in an elevator and emerged into a room whose floor was a disk enclosed in a totally transparent, fifty-foot hemisphere. The floor was resilient plastic, as black as the sky above. The domes of the lunar base were spread out below, gleaming in Earthshine. Beyond them, a ship drifted up from the landing bays, its viewports glowing like sparks in the night, its ion drive flickering with purple fire.

"This place used to be a restaurant for the tourists," the woman in the black jump suit explained. "That was before the tourist industry died out. If you're interested, there's a telescope over there, shows you the landing site of the first manned flight from Earth, back in century-twenty. Take a look."

Moved by curiosity, Aton went and peered into the antique eyepiece. He saw a dusty lunar sea pockmarked with human footprints, a spidery, four-legged platform that seemed to be the lower half of a landing module. "Hard to believe it's just been lying out there in the vacuum for four hundred years," he said.

She gave a short, sharp laugh. "It hasn't. It's a

fake. The real landing site's several hundred miles away." She sat down and folded her arms. All her movements were quick and precise, matching the way she spoke. "It doesn't make any difference. Tourists weren't interested in it, anyway."

Aton frowned at her, then looked around at the rest of the room. All the furnishings had been salvaged from space vehicles: acceleration couches, map tables, even a complete navigation console. The place was littered with gadgets: holo viewers, tape players, transceivers, translators. He picked his way across and sat down on the edge of a couch opposite her. "Why did you bring us up here?"

She gestured toward Srndhi. The Xest was lingering nervously beside the open elevator door. "He interests me. Can he talk, or is his translator malfunctioning, or what?"

"As a Xest, 'he' is really an 'it,'" Aton pointed out.

She shrugged. "Whatever." Her eyes made quick, darting movements. "You haven't answered the question."

"Before we have a conversation, I'd like to know who I'm dealing with. Are you a law-enforcement official?"

She gave a short, sharp laugh. "Shit no. I'm a systems analyst. Just about the last one left."

"Then why did you show up in the police department?"

"I show up wherever there's something interesting." She leaned forward, resting her sharp elbows on her knees. "I collect data. You understand? Anything that's new, or not known." She glanced again at

Srndhi. "Has he—it—come to replace the ambassador?"

Aton shifted back on the couch, making himself more comfortable while still watching her carefully. "No. My Xest friend hoped to get the ambassador's help, in fact—to present a proposal to the Federation government."

Her eyes narrowed. "You talk like there's a big roomful of politicians somewhere, listening to depositions, making speeches, passing legislation."

"I assume there must be some sort of central congress."

She shook her head. "Wrong." She turned in her seat. "Tomas?" She looked over her shoulder.

A large figure had been standing unnoticed in the shadows. He walked forward into the light. He had golden hair, broad shoulders, a square jaw, and clear blue eyes. His tanned, muscled chest was bare above tight black pants. "Something you want?" he asked, pausing beside the woman.

"I need a drink. For you?" She looked at Aton.

He hesitated. "I don't think—"

"You're acting paranoid. If I wanted to drug you, there's a dozen easier ways. I control all the life-support systems up here, understand? All I'm interested in is gathering data. Period." She spread her hands. "I don't often have visitors, and I won't drink alone."

"All right. Is there something made locally? Alcohol based?"

"Sure." She nodded to the brawny man, and he ambled away. "Meantime, tell your Xest friend to stop hanging around like that."

"Srndhi," Aton called, "you may as well join us."

"That's his name, huh? I'm Samantha Smith." She leaned forward and held out her hand.

He clasped it. Her palm was small but her grip was tight. "Aton Five," he told her.

"Spell it."

He did so, amused by her air of intent interest.

"From Hvee?" She nodded to herself. "Only place I know where family names are number-coded for status."

"You've been there?" Aton asked in surprise.

"Hell no. Never been anyplace except here. But I told you, I collect data." She tilted her head and pointed to a socket half hidden by her short black hair.

"You're a Sim?"

She laughed. "No, hundred percent human. Natural-born, in fact. This is just an implant for data input." She looked up as Tomas returned, carrying two glasses. "Tom, now, *he's* a Sim. All aluminum under that pseudoflesh."

"That's right," said Tomas, grinning cheerfully as he handed Aton one of the glasses.

"A handsome one, though, you got to admit." She stood up, kissed him on the cheek, and ran her hand across his naked, hairless chest. Then she took her drink out of his hand, patted his ass, and sat back in her chair. He walked slowly back into the shadows.

She turned her attention to Srndhi, as he climbed up onto the couch beside Aton. "So what brings you here?" she said casually to the Xest.

"I have come—" Srndhi began, then stopped.

"Yeah, I figured you could speak," she said. "So why were you clamming up on me like that?"

"One has reason for caution," the Xest answered. "Many unpleasant experiences in this human colony, culminating in detention and arrest."

"Arrest? I've already erased that. I viewed the tape of the incident before I went down and found you. You people don't understand the law here, that's all. Just remember, you never, ever, lay a hand on anyone. Period."

"You leave them in peace to rot in their own miserable filth, is that it?" said Aton.

She looked at him coolly. "Sure, if that's what they want. This is a totally free society. Only two rules: you don't interfere with your neighbor, and you respect private property."

"This system," the Xest spoke. "Has a purpose?"

She shrugged. "Freedom is its own purpose. Generally, it encourages growth, wealth, innovation."

"And yet one sees decay, poverty, and despair."

She took a sip of her drink and slid sideways in her chair, resting her head against one of its arms. "We're in a down-cycle. Every culture has phases of prosperity and decline. There's a lot of deadwood right now. It'll die off; new growth will take its place. What's the alternative? Start some social programs and build a bureaucracy that absorbs half the wealth so it can redistribute the other half?"

"Even that would bring a reduction of pain," said the Xest.

"Short-lived, because it would lead to stagnation. Look, I'm not interested in debating with you. This is the system that got us into space, spread us half-way across the galaxy. You can't argue with results like that."

"But that's exactly the point," Aton said. The drink was already spreading warmth through him, restoring his determination. "Human growth is completely out of hand, to the point where it's threatening other intelligent species."

She shrugged. "Competition for resources is natural."

"Natural for animals that lack any code of ethics. Haven't we evolved past that?"

She set down her drink and leaned forward. "The galaxy is just like an ecosystem, only bigger. In any ecosystem, there's competition for survival. If you restrain growth of one species, another takes its place."

"But the debt!" Srndhi complained.

"Right, I had a few discussions with your ambassador about that concept," she said. She drained her glass and set it down. "It's a neat idea—if you're into staring at your own navel. Contemplation of the infinite cellular unity of entities, et cetera, ad nauseam."

"All right," said Aton, "I can see there's no point in arguing with you. But there has to be some way the Xest race can put their case to the Federation."

"I am an emissary from my people," Srndhi explained. "For years I have journeyed, gathering data. I have observed much. If I am able to communicate with your government, I believe I may appeal not only to their intelligence, but to their humanity."

She laughed. "Humanity. That's funny. The whole administrative system is artificial intelligence. Any 'humanity' it has was programmed into it centuries ago."

Aton stared at her. "All the decisions of government are preprogrammed?"

"It's more flexible than that. It's self-modifying; only the precepts are fixed. If you want to make your case, all you have to do is talk into that terminal." She gestured to a console. "But even that isn't necessary. Tom? You've been storing this conversation?"

"Yes, Samantha." His mellow voice came from behind her.

"Copy it through to Central." She turned back to Aton. "Anything else you want to add, that you haven't already said?"

Aton stared at her. "Just like that?"

"Sure."

"I have in fact prepared a statement," Srndhi said. "It is as follows. My species petitions your species for self-restraint." It spoke slowly, with dignity. "Since mankind's survival in the galaxy is now assured, one should be concerned now with the quality, not the quantity, of life. Instead of biological growth, there is a need for intellectual and ethical growth. The first step must be to end genetic modification, which causes great harm and suffering not only in alien ecosystems, but to the human hybrids that are created." The Xest paused and gestured toward Aton. "My companion has personal testimony of the hardship experienced by one who is genetically less than human."

Samantha looked at Aton with frank curiosity. "You mean, you grew from a splice?"

"Second-generation," he told her stiffly. "In fact, I am a half-breed."

"Half human, and half what?"

"Minion."

She raised her eyebrows. "Interesting. But Central already has complete data on that planet; an individual case history is meaningless." She thumbed a button on the console. "Response, please."

"Petition denied." The voice was neuter, and without inflection.

She turned back to them and shrugged. "See what I mean? What you're asking for is state-imposed restraint. In other words, coercion. That's a violation of first principles."

Aton stared at her for a long moment. He stood up. "You say you're human," he said, "but you talk like a machine." He clenched his fist. "Don't you understand—"

"You're forgetting where you are," she told him. Her expression was cold. "Don't ever talk to me like that."

Aton tried to will the tension out of his muscles. He turned abruptly and strode to the curved glass wall. He stood there, staring out, taking slow, measured breaths.

"If there's something more specific you want," Samantha said from behind him, "I'd be willing to do a deal."

Aton said nothing.

She turned to Srndhi. "You said you've been gathering data, didn't you? You have a database in your ship, right?"

"That is so."

"I'll give you something you want, for a copy of everything you've got."

Aton turned, still angry. "Why don't you just steal it? You're obviously in control of all the systems, here. You can do anything you like."

"Not true." She shook her head. "We have our own ethics. We trade; we don't steal. And no way could I tamper with Central. No one's ever been able to hack that code. So, name your price."

"All right," said Aton. "I want someone who's being held here. A woman. A Minionette."

Samantha gave him a prurient smile. "What's this—a family relationship?"

He glared at her. "That information is not for sale."

"Well, excuse me. Go on."

"She was sent from Minion to your gene labs, in a coded ship, against her will. I don't know why."

"Just a minute." She stood and strode to another data terminal. She typed codes on a keyboard. "Interesting," she said, half to herself.

After a moment, she turned back to Aton. "There's a standard agreement. Every fifty years, any planet with genetically modified colonists must submit a representative sample for testing. Just so we have data on coding errors and mutations."

"Testing? What does that mean?"

"Nothing you should worry about. Takes a few weeks, and then the specimen—person—is returned. Seems Minion was delinquent; should have submitted a sample a couple years back."

"I see," said Aton. "So they used Malice because she was an embarrassment, and she happened to have her own transit capsule, so they didn't even have to pay for a Federation ship. It was convenient for them, and it put her out of the way."

"I could get you in to see her, if you want." She paused thoughtfully. "She was sent against her will? She'd verify that?"

"Of course."

"It's been a while since I checked the labs. It's a separate installation; no surveillance links. The guy that's running them is pretty weird; wouldn't hurt to pay a routine visit. I'd do that for you for free. Just to satisfy my curiosity."

"In that case," said Srndhi, "I offer my database to you freely, in return, in the continuing hope that, despite everything you have said, it may yet bring enlightenment to you. As it did to Aton Five."

"I'll accept that offer," she said, "although when it comes to enlightening me, you're going to be disappointed. But let's stop by the labs first."

"You said they are controlled by someone. A person, not an artificial intelligence," Aton said.

"Right." She touched the socket in her neck reflexively and closed her eyes for a moment, as if searching for something. Then she looked up and smiled apologetically. "For a second, I couldn't place the guy's name, and I don't like it when I can't track data, even when it's trivial. It won't mean anything to you," she went on, "but his name's Bedeker."

CHAPTER 13 _____

The ground vehicle rolled swiftly along a narrow highway that linked the main domes with the gene labs. Tomas, the tall, handsome Sim, sat at the controls; Aton sat with Srndhi and Samantha Smith in a passenger section at the rear.

"You seem to have free access to any equipment you need," Aton said, taking in the size of the vehicle and its comprehensive instrumentation.

She shrugged. "I have valuable skills, so Central gives me what I need."

"The persons on level seventeen," said Srndhi, "who were selling their body parts. One presumes their skills are less valuable."

"They don't have *anything* of value. That's their whole problem."

"But surely, they could acquire skills," Srndhi persisted. "They could be educated."

"Maybe. But they didn't choose to go that route." She glanced through the front window. "We're almost at the labs. Should be there in another minute or so."

"In the recreation dome," said Aton, "I was told that your entire population is illiterate."

"Just about," she agreed. "It's way out of fashion to teach your kids to read."

"I suppose you'd call it coercion," Aton went on, "to sit some people down in a room with one of your robots and *make* them learn to read."

"Yes," she said. "That's exactly what I'd call it."

There was a beep from the vehicle's control panel. "Please state your entry authorization code," said a synthetic voice.

Samantha moved across to the console and read a string of numerals into it. A large door slid slowly open in a perimeter wall surrounding the labs.

"What about you?" Aton asked her. "How did you acquire your knowledge?"

"My folks were systems analysts. It's a family tradition. I picked it up." She hesitated. "Tell you the truth, I wish more people would get educated. I get tired of having no one but Central and the Sims to talk to." She shrugged. "Still, I can't change the way people are."

A large airlock door opened in the dome housing the labs, just ahead.

"I sense the Bedeker consciousness," Srndhi said suddenly.

"So the old guy is still alive," said Samantha. "Interesting."

"The name sounds so familiar," said Aton. "Although—I feel as if I'm remembering it from somewhere far away. It's as if . . ." He trailed off, frowning.

The vehicle entered the airlock and the outer door slid shut behind them. After a short wait for pressurization, the inner door opened and the vehicle edged forward, stopping in a small parking area beside some large liquid storage tanks. The interior of the dome was bright with light, but a maze of partitions hid most of its contents from view.

"Hey, Bedeker," Samantha spoke into a communicator. "Surprise. You got visitors. You listening?" She paused and waited, but there was no reply. "Guess we have to walk from here on," she said. "You know, I haven't been in here in years; since I was a kid."

"Wait." Srndhi held up one of its legs. "There is danger."

"What?"

"The Bedeker consciousness—" Srndhi broke off, ran toward the control panel, jumped up onto it, and used its legs to flip a series of switches.

"Hey," Samantha shouted, "what the hell are you doing?"

Srndhi lifted a metal flap on the panel and pressed a large button beneath. The rumble of the vehicle's power plant rose to a shrill whine. The floor started vibrating.

There was a dazzling white flash, a loud concussion, and the vehicle rocked violently. Aton was thrown onto the floor, temporarily blinded by the light.

"We are being attacked," Tomas stated.

"I sensed it in the Bedeker consciousness," Srndhi

explained. "There was no time to tell you. Fortunately, the codes to erect the defense screen for this vehicle were in the Samantha Smith consciousness. Thus, one was able to act."

"Tomas!" Samantha shouted. "Get online to Central. Call security in here."

"I just did," he stated calmly.

"Can we get back out of the dome?" Aton asked.

"The exit doors are not responding," Tomas told him.

"The shield should protect us," said Samantha. "What did he use—some sort of energy beam?"

"I think so," said Tomas. "Without the shield, it would have knocked out all systems in the vehicle. At the very least, you would have eventually died from suffocation. Central doesn't monitor this area, so it would have looked like an accident caused by system failure."

"Jesus." Her face was pale and her eyes were wide. She hugged her arms across her body. "And you think Bedeker knows you?" she said to Aton.

He shook his head. "I can't pin it down. In any case, you didn't tell him who you were bringing here with you."

"You're right." She shook her head. "This kind of shit I don't need."

The main dome lighting suddenly died, and dim emergency glow-panels came to life. "Central has cut microwave power transmission to the dome from the SPS," Tomas said. He paused. Faintly, an abrasive scraping noise was audible. "Emergency units have already reached the dome and are cutting through its outer shell. But they'll have to install a temporary seal before they come through the inner wall, to avoid breaching the integrity of the dome. Most of the life forms in here require constant pressurization."

"Malice," Aton murmured to himself.

"She is present," Srndhi told him. "With many others." The Xest waved a leg in distress. "There is more pain in this place. Much more."

"It should be safe to exit the vehicle if we use suits," said Tomas. "They're sufficient protection against small weapons, and Bedeker doesn't have power, now, for anything bigger."

Samantha nodded. "All right." She opened a locker at the rear and pulled out suits for herself, Aton, and Tomas. "There's nothing that'd fit you," she told Srndhi. "I guess you better stay here."

"Provided you do not move too far, I can scan your thoughts and respond via radio," the Xest said.

"Good enough. And thanks, by the way, for putting that shield up." She flashed the alien a quick, shy smile, then zippered her suit and helped Aton into his. "Okay, switch on the power," she told him. "Red button, there. Everything else is voice-activated, and it's fully waldoed. Feel it?"

Aton flexed his muscles experimentally. Microsystems in the suit amplified every movement.

"There's a stunner and a small projectile weapon built into the right arm," she told him. "Feel the two levers down inside the glove? To activate either one, you pull it—and tell the suit 'fire' at the same time."

"Understood," said Aton.

"I'm killing the vehicle defense screen long enough for us to exit," said Tomas. He turned to Srndhi. "You know how to restore it, if you want to."

Srndhi moved back to the control panel. "I am ready."

The hatch opened and Aton followed Samantha out of the vehicle, his breathing sounding loud inside his helmet. Tomas came last, and closed the hatch behind him. The vehicle's shield snapped back on, bathing it in a pale glow.

Walkways between the partitions were lost in shadow. "Need more light," said Aton. Obediently, his suit switched on two headlights mounted either side of his helment. He turned his head and a circle of radiance moved across the scene in front of him, bleaching the colors.

"Proceed toward the center of the dome," Srndhi told him over the radio.

Aton and Samantha moved forward cautiously, with Tomas bringing up the rear. Aton found himself in a long walkway between a series of compartments. Cages, he realized. He turned his head and humanoid figures screeched in fear, cringing from the beam of light as it shone at them through metal bars. He glimpsed a monstrous thing with six legs, like a human centipede created by growing three torsos atop one another. The creature's face was shrunken and wrinkled, covered with hair.

"What the hell is this?" said Samantha.

"I guess Bedeker didn't want you to find out," Aton said.

They moved forward. The next cage contained an elephantine freak with a gross, bulbous body and stumpy legs. After that was a sealed tank full of yellow gas. Blind, emaciated creatures with flippers blundered around, leaving wet smears on the glass.

"This is monstrous," said Samantha. "Bedeker has gotten completely out of hand."

"You mean freaks and mutants have a right to freedom, too?" said Aton.

"Modification's a tough question," she said, ignoring his sarcasm. "Always has been. Does a gene have rights? Obviously not. But the creature that grows out of it does."

"You could avoid the whole problem if you outlawed human code-splicing to begin with," Aton pointed out. He shone his light at a family of miniature hominids, each eighteen inches high, climbing the bars of their cage like monkeys.

"You can pass all the laws you like," she said. "People always find a way to do what they want. Some questions are a matter for individual conscience. In a gray area, like modifications, we don't interfere so long as the work has no direct effects on our citizens. The gene labs are a private operation, and always have been."

They reached an intersection with another walkway. It was lined with more cages.

"Turn left," Srndhi said over the radio. "The Bedeker consciousness is located close by."

"What's in his mind?" Aton asked.

"It is difficult to say. There are many minds, all

shouting their thoughts. One senses his anger and frustration."

Aton and Samantha moved past more compartments, these containing life forms that were half human, half animal. Aton saw men covered in coarse, drooping skin-flaps like feathers, fluttering uselessly as they ran to and fro behind the bars and made plaintive bleating noises. There were hooved creatures, a woman whose head was a leathery tube, and some Siamese triplets, their arms joined with shiny pink webs of skin.

"None of this has any application," Samantha said. She sounded angry and confused. "It's sadism."

"Turn right," Srndhi told Aton. "You should see an enclosed area of some kind."

"Anything behind us?" Samantha asked Tomas.

"No. It's clear."

"What's Central doing? Do they have robots in the dome yet?"

"They've installed a temporary door in the hole they cut in the outer wall. They're repressurizing the boundary layer and testing for leakage. In a few minutes they should be able to cut through the inner wall. They're also trying to figure how the main airlock systems have been inactivated. But that will be easier to fix once they're inside."

"Look up ahead," said Aton. "This must be what Srndhi meant."

There was a small box-shaped building surrounded by liquid-gas tanks and freeze-storage containers. The building had no windows, and its steel door was closed.

"We should wait for help," said Samantha. "Anyone crazy enough to grow these freaks, I don't want to deal with him on our own."

Aton ignored her. He strode to the door, grabbed its handle, and pulled. The waldos in his suit whined. The metal wall of the building groaned and bulged outward. There was a ripping noise, and he tore the door out of its frame.

Aton threw it aside. He started into the building.

There were more cages here—smaller ones, measuring perhaps six feet wide by three feet high. Each contained a human figure, some of them lying unconscious, others pressing their faces to the bars. All were infected with degenerative diseases. Many were blind; others were literally rotting away, bones poking out through their corroded flesh.

Aton swung the beams of his lights. He saw microsurgery equipment and an operating table; laser tools, an elaborate laboratory, and an electron microscope. At the opposite end of the cluttered space was a living area containing a bed, a table, and shelves of data disks. A man was standing there surrounded by half-a-dozen diseased freaks on their hands and knees, shackled in chains.

The man was tall, thin, with a neatly trimmed beard. Aton stared at his face. He was sure he had never seen it before, yet it was as familiar as the man's name. "Bedeker," he said.

The man said nothing. He stood calmly as Samantha and Tomas followed Aton into the room.

"Consider yourself under arrest, Bedeker." The

transducer in Samantha's suit amplified her voice, making the creatures in chains cover their ears. They cowered beside Bedeker's feet like dogs that had been trained to obey. Most of their bodies were covered with sores and chancres. Their eyes showed an animal stupidity.

"You're interfering in something you don't understand," the bearded man said quietly. "You should never have come here."

"You're out of your mind," said Samantha, "that's all I need to understand. Why'd you do it—do you get off on causing pain?"

Bedeker smiled. "God is pain. I'm merely his agent."

"You inhuman son-of-a-bitch." She moved toward him, a bulky, menacing figure in the combat suit.

"The universe is inhuman," Bedeker answered her. "It creates life merely to torture it with a million forms of disease and death. And that's called evolution. Life is an *obscenity*. Do you see?"

"All I see is you in long-term psychiatric care."

"You're wrong," he told her.

Before she could touch him, his knees buckled, and he collapsed onto the floor.

"His consciousness has gone," Srndhi's voice came over the radio link.

"You mean he's dead?" said Aton.

"Not—precisely. The body is dead. His consciousness has undergone a displacement."

Samantha kneeled beside the figure on the floor and touched the body with a sensor that extended from her left glove. "God damn," she muttered. "No vital signs."

"Central's bots are now in the dome," Tomas reported. "I've told them to send a medicomp."

Samantha shook her head. "Too late." She backed away from one of the chained freaks that was sniffing blindly at her, its face covered in a rotting brown fungus.

"What happened to him?" Aton asked.

"He dropped dead, right in front of us, that's all I know. Let's get the hell out and let the bots clean this up."

"You're forgetting," said Aton, "I came here looking for someone."

Samantha stared at him through the visor of her suit. "You mean you still want to find her, after what you've seen in here?"

"She can't have been in the labs for more than a day," said Aton. "She may still be unharmed."

"One still senses the Minionette consciousness," Srndhi told him. "One cannot discern her physical state, however. Proceed out of the building. Turn right."

Aton left without a word. He strode out of the doorway past the lines of cages. Police and military robot units were moving in, but he ignored them. He moved quickly, swinging the lights from side to side.

"You are near," said Srndhi.

Aton passed a cage of lizard things with distorted faces, then a group of mutants whose legs had never grown below the knee. The next cage seemed empty; but when he shone the lights into it, he saw something red gleaming at the bottom, just behind the bars.

He stopped and stared, afraid to move forward. The creature in the cage sensed the light and began to stir. The redness shifted and shimmered—red hair, framing a pale face. She sat up, blinking in the glare.

Aton ran to the bars. "Malice," he said softly, staring in at her.

CHAPTER 14 _____

They took her back to the main Luna complex and laid her body on a stainless-steel table under bright white lights. Tomas moved methodically, inserting thin metal probes. He paused to check readouts on a control panel.

"Any sign of tampering?" Aton found it hard to keep the tension out of his voice as he stared at her stretched out before him, silver needles embedded in the ivory skin.

"The full analysis takes several minutes." Tomas made some adjustments, then paused, waiting.

"I really feel no different from before," Malice said, turning her green eyes toward him.

"But you told us Bedeker drugged you at one point."

"Only when my capsule landed, and I was transferred."

"There are residual traces of an anesthetic," Tomas confirmed, inspecting hard copy emerging from a slot. "But nothing toxic."

"Bedeker could have done anything to you while you were unconscious," Aton persisted.

"But I wasn't out for long. And when I woke up, he was just . . . measuring me."

Aton imagined Bedeker's hands on her body, examining, feeling, and probing. Anger swelled inside him.

Malice sensed it and breathed in sharply. The muscles in her abdomen tensed, and her nipples stiffened. She shifted on the table.

"Lie still," Tomas reminded her.

She averted her eyes. "I'm sorry. I forgot."

Aton smiled grimly. "Your emotional responses certainly haven't been altered."

"You said that Bedeker put you in confinement immediately after the physical examination?" Tomas asked her.

She turned her attention to the Sim. "Yes. He told me that there would be further adjustments later. Then he put me in that cage, and nothing else happened until Aton found me."

Aton frowned. "Bedeker told you he planned to make *further* adjustments?"

She shook her head, making her red hair shimmer under the lights. "Maybe he just said 'adjustments.' I can't remember. I was still groggy from the drug."

The monitoring unit chimed, signifying that the analysis was complete. Tomas scanned the hardcopy. "There's no evidence of any biological interference." He passed the long web of paper to Aton. "See for yourself."

Aton glanced at the itemization of cell analyses and blood levels. "If your equipment confirms that nothing happened, then I guess I believe it."

"That's not what I said," Tomas corrected him. "I said there was no evidence. Much of Bedeker's research was state-of-the-art. It's conceivable that he exposed her to some process with subtle long-term effects, impossible to diagnose at this point." He went to Malice and started pulling the needles out of her body.

"But you don't think that's likely," said Aton.

"No, I don't."

The last of the probes was removed, and Malice sat up on the table. "I'm cold," she said, hugging her arms across her breasts. "Is there anything I can wear?"

"I will give you one of Samantha's suits," said Tomas, powering down the diagnostic unit. "Come with me."

A little later Malice walked into Samantha's circular living module, under the glass hemisphere. Watching the Minionette, Aton found it hard not to touch her. The suit that Tomas had given her was cut to fit Samantha's smaller, slimmer build; it clung to Malice's thighs, graphically outlined her hips and buttocks, and was stretched tight across the swelling of her breasts.

Srndhi moved forward to greet her.

"Malice, this is my Xest friend who helped me to escape from Minion, and brought me to Luna," Aton explained. "Srndhi also saved our lives when Bedeker attacked our vehicle in the gene labs."

"I'm grateful to you," she told the Xest, "and honored to meet a member of your race."

"One appreciates this expression of friendship."

Srndhi paused for a moment, as if scanning her thoughts, then turned and walked back across the black plastic floor. "Samantha has been supervising the shutdown of the labs. There is much data."

"Is there any information on how or why Bedeker died?" Aton asked.

Samantha was at one of her consoles. She looked up and disconnected a thin cable linking the terminal with her implant. "Bedeker's blood turned out to be a pharmacological grab bag." She pushed her chair back. "He was dosing himself with a broad spectrum of depressants—but nothing that would have killed him. All the vital organs were healthy, which is no surprise, since most of them had been stolen out of specimens before he put them in his zoo. Overall, there was no physical reason for him to die."

"Maybe an autonomic block," said Aton. "I've heard they can be programmed to enable a painless form of suicide."

"I agree, it's a possibility." Samantha stood up and looked at Malice. "So you're the Minionette."

"I gave her one of your suits," Tomas explained.

Samantha eyed the other woman's body. "Yeah. I more or less recognize it." A flicker of irritation showed on her face, then was erased.

"What about Bedeker's history?" Aton asked. "I'd be interested to know if there's any way he and I could have met, in the past."

Samantha looked from Malice to Aton, as if imagining the two of them coupled together. Then she seemed to wipe the subject from her mind. "Bedeker doesn't *have* a history," she said. "His claimed birthdate would make him age fifty, but there's no evidence. He could have been three times as old. He arrived on Luna thirty years back, claiming he'd made his millions from heavy-metal prospecting in the asteroid belt. He acquired a majority holding in the gene labs at a time when the stock just happened to be grossly undervalued. He took complete control of the business, changed it to a private corporation, dismissed all other employees over a period of two decades, and spent the past ten years in total isolation. You figure it out."

Aton pondered what she had said. Her story explained none of the resonances stirred by Bedeker's name. "What's happening to the labs now?"

"The specimens who were deliberately infected with incurable diseases are being put out of their misery. The healthier ones are being asked to choose between corrective surgery or transportation to worlds where conditions match their deformities."

"Commendably compassionate," Aton commented.

She gave him a vexed look. "It was Srndhi's suggestion. You'll be pleased to hear, incidentally, that Bedeker wired a lot of his equipment to self-destruct if it was tampered with. The units that went in to secure the labs were programmed for riot control, not systems analysis. They blundered into Bedeker's alarm sensors and reduced his equipment to junk. Also, before he died, he wiped his entire database. So there's no way the labs can continue operation. No one has the knowledge to put it all back together."

"One finds pleasure in this outcome," Srndhi observed, "even though the process by which it was reached involved damage and destruction."

Samantha rolled her eyes in exasperation. "Will you *please* cut out the moralizing?" She turned back to Malice and studied her as if the Minionette was still a source of some special interest. "So you survived. One of the few lucky ones. I received your whole-body analysis just now"—she touched the socket in her neck—"and it looks normal—within the parameters of your Minion genotype, that is."

"I feel fine," Malice said simply.

Once again, Samantha looked speculatively from Malice to Aton. Then she shrugged. "All right. So all that's left now is for me to access the Xest database, as promised. Shall we head on over to Srndhi's ship?" She started toward the elevator. "Tomas, you stay here and monitor the network. I'll be offline for a while."

"Yes, Samantha."

Srndhi touched Aton discreetly with the tip of one of its legs. "There is something you should know."

Aton looked down at the Xest. "What is it?"

"The Bedeker consciousness. I believe it still exists."

"Hey, come on, you guys," Samantha called from the elevator. "I thought you were ready."

"I will explain later," Srndhi said.

Finally, they were alone together. Srndhi had escorted Samantha to the Meditation Room, and had then disappeared to some other part of the Xest ship with its smaller self. Aton found himself with Malice in the control room, standing opposite her; and for a long moment, neither of them spoke.

Now that there was no one else listening or observing them, he felt inhibited and self-conscious. He wanted her as much as ever, yet he was unsure where to begin. He looked at her face, remembering all his fantasies of her, and the one night they had shared in her cabin on Minion. "I've thought a lot about you," he said, realizing as he said it that the statement sounded flat and inadequate.

"Naturally, you have been in my thoughts, also." She smiled awkwardly, but seemed unwilling to meet his eyes.

"Srndhi taught me some things, on the way here from Minion," he went on. "I don't feel the same ambivalence anymore."

"You do seem somewhat different," she agreed. Her voice sounded formal, and she made no movement toward him.

"I simply had to accept the facts." He reached out, stroked his fingertip gently down the side of her neck, then took her hand. "I want you," he told her.

She looked up at him, and her green eyes seemed full of desire. But she shook her head. "No," she told him.

He stared at her as if he couldn't believe what he had heard.

She backed away from him, shaking her head again. "I'm sorry, Aton."

He laughed. "I don't believe this."

"I too had time to think." She turned, hiding her

face from him. "I thought they would kill you on Minion. I never expected you to escape."

"What the hell does that mean? Aren't you glad that I survived?"

She shook her head. "In a way—no."

"You wanted me *dead?*" His voice rose incredulously.

She walked restlessly across the control room and looked out of the viewport. The long lunar night was gradually coming to an end, and the first rays of sunlight were outlining the peaks of the mountains in bright gold fire.

"No, of course I didn't want you to die," she said. "But I did think it was all finally over." She drew a deep breath and turned to confront him. "You're obsessed, Aton. You're dangerous. You're like a drug to me; your rage and anguish give me pure ecstasy. But your hatred extends beyond me, to everything else, even yourself. You *killed* people, on Minion, because of your feelings for me."

"I'll find a way to atone for those deaths," he said quietly.

"Even if you do, there'll still be more."

"No!" He strode across to her and grabbed her by her arms. "I tell you, I have changed."

She shook her head sadly. "You can't change. You admitted it yourself."

His grip on her tightened reflexively. "You don't know what you're talking about. I hurt other people because I couldn't live with my own stigma. But that's not the way it is, anymore."

She shook her head. "I simply can't believe that."

Her implacable refusal made him feel a sense of

outrage. For a moment he imagined forcing her to accept him. He fantasized inflicting on her the pain she was now inflicting on him, till he broke her resistance and she surrendered, admitting her need for him.

She sensed his emotions. "You tempt me," she said, "as you always have. But I have decided; it cannot be."

There was a polite tap on the door. "One regrets to intrude." It was Srndhi's voice.

Aton stepped back quickly. He retreated across the cabin, unable to speak.

"One senses that the merging of human selves does not proceed as one had hoped," the alien observed.

Aton turned and pointed at Malice. "Tell her, Srndhi." His voice was loud in the small space. "You can see in my mind. Tell her that I've changed."

Malice shook her head. "Please, Aton."

Once again he imagined himself crushing her beauty—and he saw her flinch as she sensed his rage as an erotic, physical force. But she turned away from him, refusing to acknowledge it. And without her permission and acceptance, his rage was impotent.

"Unfortunately, this is not a time for personal concerns," said the Xest. It moved into the control room, followed by its smaller self, and took its seat on the stool in front of the control panel. "One senses that Samantha Smith is even now emerging from the Meditation Room. She will join us momentarily. She has already learned much. Among these data are the facts one is about to give you. My smaller self, in charge of the ship's systems, was routinely monitoring all transmissions, including those in the telepathic spectrum. It detected a powerful beam emanating from the gene laboratories at the time of Bedeker's death."

"Srndhi, I don't even care," Aton responded. "You got what you wanted. The labs are shut down. All that matters to me right now—"

"The transmission was of the Bedeker consciousness," the Xest continued implacably. "One has calculated the coordinates to which it was directed. A distant planet named Chthon."

The word triggered something inside Aton. There was a sense of dislocation. "The prison planet," he said, and his own voice sounded strange to him.

"The Bedeker consciousness has been reconstituted there," Srndhi told him.

There were footsteps outside in the corridor, and Samantha walked in. Her face was pale and she seemed shaken. She blinked in the light and looked from Srndhi to Aton, and then to Malice.

"You have experienced enlightenment," the Xest said to Samantha.

She stood in the doorway, touching its metal frame. Then she stepped across to one of the stools and sat down heavily. "That was quite a ride," she said. She gave a strange, strained laugh. "Impressive. Very impressive."

"One has just explained to Aton about the displacement of the Bedeker consciousness," Srndhi said.

"Oh. That. Yeah." She nodded, still looking dazed.

"Xests were unaware that humans had acquired the capability for this form of telepathic transmission."

She shook her head. "News to me, too. Maybe

Bedeker figured it out himself, or maybe he stole it somehow."

"It constitutes a great danger," said Srndhi.

"You think so?" She put her hand to her forehead, still having trouble focusing on her surroundings. "Look, even if you're right, and Bedeker's resuscitated himself in Chthon somehow, seems like it's the best place for him to be. A prison planet, right? And no one in history has ever escaped from it."

"You do not understand." Srndhi moved its legs impatiently. "While you were in meditation, oneself and one's smaller self communicated with the Xest home worlds and requested records of other possible telepathic transmissions into, and from, the planet Chthon. We learned much. The planet itself possesses a powerful intelligence."

"The *planet*?" said Aton. "How can a planet be alive?"

"We think its mineral intelligence evolved in a molten metal core much as biological intelligence evolved in the ocean. It is inhuman in every sense. It regards biological life as an abomination."

"When we found Bedeker, he spouted some antilife crap that sounded like that," said Samantha.

"Correct. He and Chthon are in accord, and they have made contact with extragalactic entities that also appear to be mineral in origin. While you were emerging from meditation, we completed our analysis. Please make use of your implant to receive this data."

"Uh, sure." She gave the Xest a doubting look, but stood up and moved over to the control panel. "How—"

"A link has been prepared."

The small Xest walked forward, dragging a cable toward her.

Samantha bent forward and peered at the miniature creature. "Hey, cute," she said, accepting the cable from it. "Thanks, little guy." She plugged in, closed her eyes, and the muscles in her face relaxed.

The download only took a few seconds. She disconnected and turned to Srndhi with a strange, puzzled expression. "Even with my implant, this is kind of hard to absorb." She replaced the cable carefully on the console. "If you're right, what we're dealing with here could wipe us out. I mean, everything."

"Quite so." Srndhi paused. "One hopes you may be able to lend assistance."

CHAPTER 15 _____

The early lunar colonists had profited from a simple fact: outside of Earth's gravity well, the moon and the asteroid belt were rich in easily extracted ores. Exploration required immense investment; but once the robot-controlled mining equipment was in place, delivery of shipments by mass-driver was a trivial expense.

On Earth, Western nations had become desperate for minerals such as titanium and beryllium. The spacefaring entrepreneurs were well positioned to exploit this need, and they profited from it.

Like early oil tycoons of a previous century, they showed a maverick disregard for government regulation and conventional notions of propriety. They built themselves an unregulated society—and then took steps to make sure it would stay that way.

Internally, the lunar libertarian system was protected against subversion by an artificial intelligence that constituted the first benevolent, efficient bureaucracy in history, programmed to inhibit only those forms of human behavior that violated fundamental freedoms. Externally, however, the system was more vulnerable: an ungoverned society of diehard individualists was inevitably ill suited to fight wars.

Consequently, the colonists diverted a huge proportion of their wealth into automated military systems. The moon became more heavily fortified than any nation on Earth, harboring a vast fleet armed with every imaginable form of weapon. This overkill served its purpose: the defenses were so formidable, they never needed to be used. The weapons forever slumbered in their silos—until, centuries later, Samantha Smith passed to Computer Central the data she had received from the Xests concerning the planet Chthon and its link with mineral entities outside the galaxy.

Maintenance robots had kept the war fleet in a state of perpetual readiness. It took less than an Earth day to activate and test the dormant systems. Then, from the dead cratered face of the moon, defaced with mine workings and man-made debris from a bygone era, a hundred ships drifted outward into space, gleaming like dust motes in the sun.

Aton sat alone in an observation blister, staring out into space. This starship had lain idle for centuries; now, it was nearing lightspeed and the star images were smearing into rainbowed teardrops, as if they were being viewed through a distorting prism.

Samantha walked in and paused behind him. She stood quietly for a minute, then slid past him and sat down on the only other chair in the tiny compartment. "I guess this is nothing new to you," she said. Her voice sounded more relaxed than he remembered it; more reflective.

Aton didn't answer. He had retreated inward since his confrontation with Malice the previous day, and had spent most of his time in solitude, taking no part in the preparations for the mission.

"Funny thing is," Samantha went on, "I've never seen any of this. Never even traveled to Earth. Spent my whole damn life on Luna, wired into the net. Gathering data secondhand."

Aton turned and looked at her. The spectral colors touched her pale skin, softening the tensions in her face. There was a shyness behind her abrupt mannerisms.

She tilted her chair back and stared up through the curved panels. "I hope to god the data on Chthon is wrong," she said. "And you know, it still might be. I mean, there's no way to verify anything. The Xests won't share their technology for tapping the telepathic spectrum, so we just have to take their word for what they heard."

"Your Computer Central certainly seemed convinced," said Aton. He spoke slowly, finding it an effort to make conversation.

She laughed. "Yeah. More or less. Never thought I'd see it, all the old defense systems mobilized. We have enough firepower to vaporize the whole damn planet, if that's what it'll take."

Aton looked up sharply. "That—wouldn't be right."

She swiveled her chair and looked at him with her head tilted to one side. "What?"

"There are people on that planet. They shouldn't have to die."

"A few thousand criminals," she pointed out. "And we're talking about saving billions of lives."

Aton looked puzzled and unhappy. "I suppose you're right. I don't know, I_keep getting these sudden flashes—"

"Déjà-vu? Flashbacks?"

"More like flashes forward." But there was no way he could explain to her his strange sense of predestination. He sighed. "Forget it."

She looked again at the view. The star-streaks were growing into lines, rainbow-hued, radiating from an indistinct black circle directly ahead. The circle was slowly expanding, engulfing the colors around it. "Approaching lightspeed," Samantha said.

Aton said nothing, lost again in his thoughts.

"You know, this ship was built for civilian use, originally, before it was militarized and put in storage. It was designed for pleasure cruises. The observation blisters were for couples to hold hands and watch the stars. Romantic, huh?" She smiled at him.

He tried to read her expression. "Yes, it must have been."

She brushed her hair back from her forehead. It was a shy, awkward gesture. "What about you, Aton? Do you ever get romantic?"

He tried to imagine what it would be like to hold her. In some ways, she seemed childlike. He had never been with a woman like her.

She leaned forward, moving with a self-conscious lack of grace. She touched him tentatively, slid her hand inside the neck of his shirt, then kissed him clumsily on the mouth.

After a moment, he moved his arm around to embrace her. She lay beside him, her body feeling tense.

Abruptly, she pulled away. "Forget it, I can tell you're not really interested." She sat back in her chair. "You're still thinking about your Minionette." She forced a laugh. "That woman really has her hooks in you, doesn't she?"

Aton was quiet for a moment. "Have you ever had sex with a human male, as opposed to a Sim?" he asked her.

"Me? Yeah, sure." She paused, as if remembering. "Used to see a lot of different guys, a few years back. But they were such stupid shits. Tomas gives me all I want."

"Really?"

She drew a shaky breath. "Well, he did till I went through that goddamn Xest Meditation Room. I had my whole life figured out, everything under control, and then zap." She stood up. "Look, I'm sorry, I didn't mean to dump this on you."

"You don't have to apologize for being human," he told her.

She looked out of the blister. The fuzzy black circle had grown so large, it now seemed poised to absorb the entire ship. "Hey, how about that. First time in my life, I'm going into FTL."

He reached out toward her. "Samantha—"

She avoided him. "I told you, forget it." She started for the door, then paused. "By the way," she said, trying to sound casual. "Srndhi told me to tell you. Your girlfriend wants to see you, down in her cabin."

She ducked out before Aton had time to answer.

Aton knocked on the door. His throat felt tight and

his pulse was unnaturally fast. He cursed Malice for the emotional power she still had over him, then cursed himself for still being so helpless to control it.

"Come in." Her voice was so faint, he barely heard it through the aluminum panel.

He walked in. In the days when the ship had been used for tourist travel, this would have been one of the most expensive staterooms. He saw ornate mirrors, aluminum furniture disguised to look like antiques, crystal light fixtures, a synthetic carpet, genuine wooden veneers.

Malice was sitting on the edge of the bed. Her cheeks were flushed and her eyes looked sore. She clasped her hands nervously in front of her and stared up at Aton without speaking.

He closed the door carefully behind him. "I gather you told Srndhi—"

"We talked together for a while," she said. Her voice sounded shaky and tense. "I didn't even know he was on the ship. He said his smaller self is in control of his ship, and he wanted to be here with Samantha to be sure that the systems . . ." She stopped herself short. "I suppose you know all this."

Aton stepped forward. He gestured impatiently. "Tell me why you wanted to see me."

"Srndhi and I talked."

"Yes, you just told me that."

"All right!" Her voice was suddenly shrill. "Can't you see I don't know how to say it?"

"What? *What* is it you don't know how to say?"

"That I was wrong." She said the words haltingly, as if it was a physical effort. "You may be right. Maybe you have changed."

He absorbed the meaning of what she had just said, and the tension flowed out of him. A growing warmth took its place, spreading through his body. He felt himself coming back to life.

"But I'm still not sure!" she warned him. "Srndhi can look into your head, and see every detail. I can only sense your feelings. There's no way I can know—" She broke off and cried out as Aton threw her backward on the bed.

"Take this off." His voice was loud. He pointed at the zipper of the jump suit.

She stared up at him uncertainly. "But—"

"Take it off!" He glared at her.

She reached for the zipper and slowly pulled it down. "What are you going to do?"

"I'm going to vent my anger on you," told her, "for doubting me."

His rage was focused on her like a hot, bright light. Her muscles went limp as her psyche transmuted the fury into passion.

She closed her eyes and pulled the jump suit open, exposing herself for him to use in whatever way he wished.

Later, she lay passively in his arms. He had beaten her and he had ravished her for what felt like hours, yet he was still not sated. He had stopped, finally, because he was too tired to go on.

"Promise me something, Aton," she told him quietly.

He touched welts that he had raised with the edge of his belt. Already, they were fading, healed by her modified immune system. "What do you want?" he asked.

"Promise me that from now on, no innocent people will suffer. You will take out your anger on me alone."

He nodded. "Yes, I think I can promise that."

She sighed, drugged with her own fulfillment. "I think I believe you." She turned to face him. "Do you forgive me, now, for rejecting you, and for doubting you?" Her eyes seemed to look deep into him, demanding the truth.

"I—think I do," he said cautiously.

She sat up in the bed. Her face was intensely serious. "No. Don't ever forgive me."

He looked at her in puzzlement, unable to make sense of this sudden reversal.

"You must *always* resent me, *always* feel that anger gnawing inside you," she told him. "If you forgive me, you might start to love me; and if your love was as intense as your hate, I have no doubt that it would kill me."

He remembered what she had once told him, about the penalties on her home world for men who injured their wives with love. He nodded slowly. "All right."

"Tell me what you thought about me, in the last twenty-four hours, after I rejected you." Her expression was still intensely serious.

"I—wanted to punish you, for the way you had hurt me. I imagined hurting you in return."

"Ah, yes." She slumped back down and let out a long, slow sigh, savoring his vindictiveness. "And was there more? Surely, you must have thought of other ways of taking your revenge."

"It's true, I did. I imagined forcing you to your

knees, making you pledge yourself and promise never to defy me again."

A devious look came into her eyes. "I still haven't really done that, have I? Maybe I'm still not quite ready. Suppose I told you I don't want to." She licked her lips. Her breathing was fast. "What would you do to me?"

"Bitch!" He slapped her face.

She tilted her chin. "That didn't hurt at all."

His anger fed strength into his weary arms. He seized her, hit her again—then fell on her with renewed desire.

"If you truly want to possess me, Aton," she told him later, "there's a game we can play."

He was lying beside her, half asleep. "A game? I'm too tired for games."

"Just listen, then, and I'll describe it to you. There is a custom, on Minion, between a woman and her lover, when they are not yet married but wish to symbolize their bond." And she described what she had in mind.

"But I doubt the ship's stores have the materials you need," he said, when she finished.

"Let's find out." She seemed playful and alert, as if she had been revitalized by all the abuse he had inflicted on her. "Samantha's man-robot; what was his name?"

"Tomas."

"Yes, Tomas. When he assigned me this room, he told me to call for anything I wanted." She rolled across the bed and pressed the button on an intercom. "Tomas? Are you there?"

There was a moment's pause. "Yes?" The Sim's voice emerged from a concealed loudspeaker.

"Tomas, I need something." She looked at Aton and smiled wickedly. "I need several feet of thick, strong twine."

There was a moment of puzzled silence. "We have synthetic tape," he answered. "Would that do? Or steel wire, in the maintenance section."

"Wire. That would be even better. Thin, strong wire. Oh, and something to cut it with."

"Very well. I'll be there shortly."

"You're crazy," Aton told her.

"No more so than you. And would you have it any other way?" She looked at him challengingly.

"No," he admitted.

A few minutes later, Tomas delivered a coil of fine, flexible wire and a pair of cutters. Malice received it from him at the door without bothering to conceal her nakedness.

"I know he's only a Sim," Aton told her after Tomas had left, "but there's no need to display yourself like that."

"You mean, you don't want anyone else to see my body?"

"That's right. I don't."

"Then you'd better do what I've suggested, to remind me that I'm yours."

She stood passively, still naked, and he began winding the wire around her body. "Twine would really have been better," she said. "The coarseness of it provides such exquisite torment. On the other hand, this digs deeper into my skin."

"Is it too tight?" he asked.

"No! Make it tighter—especially around my thighs, and my breasts. Each time I breathe in, I want it to grip me, reminding me of you holding me fiercely."

He did as she said, spiraling it around her body, although leaving her arms free. Finally he secured the end and cut the wire short.

She admired herself in a mirror, then went to a built-in closet. "Tomas told me there would be clothes here for me. Ah, yes." She riffled through a dozen outfits on hangers. "This, do you think?" She took out a simple one-piece dress, then quickly pulled it on. "Only you will know what I'm wearing under it, to symbolize my surrender to you." She bit her lip, her cheeks flushed with pleasure.

"Aton?" Samantha's voice intruded from the intercom.

With difficulty, he looked away from Malice. "Yes?" he asked.

"Hope I'm not interrupting anything." It was hard to tell from her tone of voice whether she meant what she said. "But if you and your Minionette come up to the control room, Srndhi has some new data."

CHAPTER 16 _____

The control room was paneled in white ceramics and brushed aluminum. Black consoles stood at intervals across the metallic floor, displaying multicolor readouts. Compared with the Xest ship, the room was ostentatious, its lavish sense of style reflecting the expansionist mentality of the Earth people who had designed it three centuries ago.

Several Sims were seated at the controls; and if the use of humanoid robots to supervise automatic systems seemed doubly redundant, that too typified the extravagance of a bygone epoch.

Samantha, Srndhi, and Tomas were seated around a huge starcube displaying the ship's trajectory across the spiral arm of the galaxy. Srndhi turned to greet Aton and Malice as they approached. "One is pleased to discern that the reconciliation has occurred," the Xest observed shrewdly.

"I'm indebted to you, Srndhi," Aton said. "Again."

"No, no. The debt was mine, and has now been repaid." It looked again at Malice, as if something about her was of special interest. "One wishes that there were time for further discussion of the mating customs of your culture," Srndhi said thoughtfully. "One experiences great curiosity over your current mode of dress."

She laughed, and her cheeks flushed pink. Since the Xest was able to see clearly into her mind, her secret bondage was no secret from the alien at all. "One day, I'll tell you," she said.

"One waits in anticipation."

Samantha had been sitting in silence, staring fixedly at the starcube. "Can we get back to business?" She glanced at Aton, then looked quickly away.

"Of course," he said.

"You see our current position." A white spot glowed one-third of the way along a blue arc cutting between the stars. "We'll reach Chthon within another seven hours. In view of the dangers, I'm wondering if you want to opt out."

Aton spread his hands. "I automatically assumed—"

"This is no time for assumptions. You could take one of the small transit capsules we're carrying, and go where you want. Home, maybe."

Aton shook his head. "I have no home. And I have to see this through. I feel a kind of . . . commitment."

Samantha turned to Malice. "How about you?" Her voice was carefully neutral.

"I will accompany Aton," she said simply.

Samantha shrugged. "Okay. Srndhi, you better brief them."

"Very well. One has succeeded in decoding more of the communication intercepted between Chthon and the extragalactic mineral entities. I assume you have heard of the phenomenon known as the Chill?"

"You mean so-called Kill-Chill radiation?" said Aton.

"Yes. Spreading from the center of the galaxy, it has caused more deaths in the past four centuries than any other natural phenomenon in recorded history. Its exact nature remains unknown, but we now find that Chthon and the other entities are engineering a modification of it designed to alter atomic structure. One effect will be to enable the formation of compounds that cannot normally exist. In particular, the combination of oxygen and fluorine."

"Alchemists used to call fluorine Phthor," Samantha put in, "from the Greek *phtheiro*, meaning destruction, because it's so highly reactive. If the structure of matter were changed to enable a compound consisting of oxygen and fluorine, carbon-based life would be impossible. Everything from vegetation to mammals would be annihilated."

"Phthor," Aton repeated to himself. The word had a strange resonance.

The Xest pressed buttons on a control panel at the side of the starcube. The display of the galaxy was replaced by the slowly rotating 3-D image of a verdant planet. "Superficially, Chthon appears an hospitable world. On its surface is a retreat known as Idyllia."

"Vacation paradise of the galactic spiral arm," Samantha said laconically.

The Xest seemed momentarily puzzled. "It is? Well, fortunately the population is small, consisting almost entirely of tourists, and their evacuation has been arranged. The caves in the interior of the planet, however, constitute a vast natural prison."

"Yes," said Aton. "I know." He had a sudden vision of rock tunnels, unbearable heat, naked convicts sweating in the garnet mines.

"Evacuation of the convict population is impractical," Srndhi went on. "Consequently one is reluctant to consider demolition of the planet, as Samantha advocates."

"I agree," said Aton. "It seems there has to be some other alternative."

"There is another way," Samantha told him. "But I don't think you'll like it. One of our ships is carrying a mass eater. That's a small kernel of collapsed matter. Asteroid miners use it to reach deep lodes, but it's tricky to handle. Once released, it accretes normal matter—eats through anything. We figure it could sink a shaft to the center of Chthon in a couple of hours."

"Our data show a large hollow chamber near the center of the planet," Srndhi explained. "The mineral intelligence is almost certainly located there. An access shaft would enable us to eradicate it."

"Personally," Samantha added, "I wouldn't want to be the one taking that elevator ride. My way would be to park a couple of AUs out, vaporize Chthon with our combined firepower, then get the hell away from there before the gamma radiation reached us."

"Can't you use remote control to guide the mass eater down to the center?" Aton asked.

"No. It creates field effects that interfere with communications. Manual control is the only option."

Aton shrugged. "All right. I'll do it."

She studied him with a kind of baffled fascination. "Why?"

"Let's just say I have a debt to pay. If I fail, you can still deal with Chthon your way."

Samantha turned to Srndhi. "You were right. You said he'd volunteer."

"One sensed the possibility." The Xest looked at Malice. "But will you accompany Aton?"

"I'm qualified as a pilot," she said. "I used to command an FTL ship. It sounds as if my skills could be useful. But in any case"—she gave him a half smile—"I've agreed to do whatever he wants."

Samantha took Aton and Malice in a small transit capsule to the cargo ship that was carrying the mass eater. The blackness of FTL space still cloaked them; the lack of stars outside the viewports induced claustrophobia.

They docked and entered. The cargo ship's utilitarian corridors were dusty and bare. For centuries, maintenance robots had been the only visitors here.

Samantha led them down several levels, following a map she had obtained from the mother ship's database. "This should be it," she said, opening a bulkhead door. Glow-panels came to life, revealing a wide, low-ceilinged storage area cluttered with crated machinery. "Yes, that looks like the containment vessel." She pointed to a metal sphere ten feet in diameter. "And that's the guidance vehicle." She indicated a forty-foot aluminum cylinder parked nearby. "Let's go look."

The interior of the guidance vehicle was crowded

with equipment. It smelled of old plastics, and the surfaces were covered with a thin, fine layer of dust. "That's the pilot's position." Samantha indicated a bank of screens arrayed in front of an acceleration couch. "The guidance engineer—meaning you, Aton—sits at this end. See, this vehicle carries the mass eater in its containment vessel, suspended at the end of a cable, at what is optimistically known as a non-destructive distance. Just in case of accidents." She gave him a thin smile. "You release the mass eater and it sinks down toward your target. It eats its way in, and you follow it on down, till you, ah, get where you're going."

Aton stared at the elaborate controls. "Waldos?" he asked.

"Kind of. Never used it myself, you understand; I'm just telling you what I got out of the database. Those handles, there, control the grapples. There's your containment-vessel release switch. The screens show your proximity to the eater. Naturally, you don't want to get too close." Again, the thin smile.

Aton stared blankly at the elaborate equipment. "I'll never learn how to use this in the time we have available."

"Sure you will." She opened a storage compartment, rummaged through its contents, and took out a small needle probe. "Here. This learning implant is all you need. Tomas will fit you with it; it'll teach you the reflexes."

Malice was inspecting the pilot's position. "They look like the manual controls of a transit capsule," she said.

"Absolutely. You'll have no problem there."

"But what I don't understand," said Aton, "is how to control the mass eater after it's released. If it consumes all forms of matter, how can we stop it from running wild?"

"You hold it in position with a powerful, shaped magnetic field," she said. "But you're right, guidance is the tricky part. Putting it back in its bottle is *especially* difficult, as I understand it." She pocketed the probe and closed the storage compartment. "Want to see the eater itself?"

They followed her out of the cylinder and across the steel deck to the metal sphere nearby. She walked around it till she reached a thick window in the side, and peered in. "Yeah, that's it. Take a peek."

Aton looked through the quartz panel. Deep in the interior of the sphere, a point of intense light was emitting an eerie, flickering purple radiance.

"It's in a magnetic bottle right now," Samantha explained from behind him. "If it wasn't for that, it would eat through the sphere and on out through the ship, accreting anything it could find."

Aton imagined the flickering point of light sinking down into Chthon, carving a smooth tunnel through the volcanic rock. A powerful feeling of déjà-vu gripped him and he saw himself in the tunnel, falling freely, spinning into a strange kind of oblivion.

Samantha was touching his shoulder, saying something.

He looked up quickly. "What?"

"I said, if you two really want to go through with this, we have to get moving. Install the learning implant, test it, and move this equipment to the unloading bay. Also, arm the guidance vehicle with explosives and defensive weapons, just in case. Are you okay?"

"I'm—fine," Aton said.

"I was thinking maybe you just realized how crazy this whole scheme is. Sure you don't want out?"

Once again he saw the tunnel down into Chthon. "No," he said. "This is what I have to do."

CHAPTER 17 _____

The guidance vehicle was in a low orbit, fifty miles above the surface of Chthon. The planet's blue-green disk filled the screen, eclipsing stars and space. Far below, against the face of the planet, Aton saw a bright point of light rising through the atmosphere.

"The last evacuation ship just lifted off," Samantha told him over the radio link. "They'll be clear in a few minutes."

She was speaking from the mother ship, parked with the rest of the fleet a hundred thousand miles out, orbiting Chthon's single moon. The body of the moon would form a natural shield, if necessary.

"We saw it," Malice acknowledged from the pilot's position in the guidance vehicle. "Let us know when to begin the approach."

Aton glanced at the downscreen. The containment vessel was clamped in position, ready to be released. Behind that, in a matching orbit, a backup ship loaded with weapons was following under automatic pilot.

Aton looked at the console in front of him. His head still ached gently from the learning probe, but it had done its job. He touched his gloved hands to the controls and sensed his new reflexes.

"Okay, go on down," said Samantha. "Maintain contact while you can. When you open the containment vessel, we may lose this link."

"May you find good fortune." It was Srndhi's voice.

The ship turned under Aton, then vibrated as Malice applied reverse thrust. "We're leaving polar orbit." Her voice sounded cool and professional, as if her yielding, erotic persona had been erased. Yet she still had time to turn in her pressure suit and flash Aton a brief smile.

The parkland and forests of Idyllia passed slowly by, far below. A glaring white expanse of cloud intruded briefly; and then they were moving across an ocean, its purple-blue expanse dotted with brown islands.

"Altitude ten miles," she told Aton.

From outside the insulated hull came the faint sound of air roaring past. The ship jerked and dipped, then settled back into its trajectory.

"Seven miles. Homing on target. Reducing velocity to mach three."

Aton felt his weight increasing; felt the contoured chair yielding beneath him.

"Target area in view."

He checked his screen and saw that the ocean terminated ahead, giving way to a wilderness area of grassy plains and hillsides.

"Mach one. One mile."

The landscape was expanding rapidly, now, in the viewscreen. A wisp of cloud flashed past. Aton saw a herd of goatlike creatures running for cover as the ship fell toward them.

"Two thousand feet. Fifty feet per second."

They were no longer plummeting; the vehicle was sinking gently, now. "Ready to release the containment vessel," Aton said. He felt strangely calm, as if the screens depicted events on some other world, unimaginably distant. But as he reached for the controls he noticed his palms were sweating inside the gloves of his pressure suit.

"Five hundred feet," said Malice. "Twenty feet per second. Ready."

Aton let his probe-learned reflexes take over. He twisted a control, pressed a switch, and watched the downscreen. The spherical containment vessel fell gently, its cable unreeling. There was a faint jolt.

"Magnetic grapples on. I'm releasing the mass eater."

"Good luck, you guys." Samantha's voice came over the radio. Then the transmission broke up with a sudden burst of static.

The eater emerged: a miniature glaring sun, cradled between invisible hands beneath the ship. It sputtered and flared, absorbing dust and air molecules into its heart of collapsed matter. It lit the landscape in stark relief, like summer lightning.

"Sink rate rising to fifty feet per second," Malice reported.

Aton felt feedback in the control handles and moved them instinctively in response. The eater neared the ground and tugged at its magnetic leash, eager to consume the soil beneath. The screens turned white, then compensated, as there was an immense, silent flash of light.

"Weapon ship still following?" Aton asked. He didn't dare look away from the screen in front of him.

"Yes, it's there." Her voice was gentler, less coolly professional, now that she had finished controlling the descent.

Gusts of dirt and vapor were swirling up. Aton switched to ultrasound and the picture cleared. The eater had adsorbed a clean cavity fifty feet deep, twenty feet in diameter. "Looks good," he reported. "Try a faster sink rate. Say, a hundred feet per second."

"One hundred," she confirmed.

The eater ripped into the planet, and the ship followed it down into the shaft it had created. In the sidescreens, Aton saw raw rock moving past. Another déjà-vu tugged at his mind—visions of caverns and lava tubes, and an endless trek through semidarkness. He blinked, trying to maintain focus. The ship rocked under him, hit by bursts of gas and dirt from the eater below. Faintly, through the insulated hull, he heard the roaring and rumbling of matter collapsing, accreting to the kernel being held so delicately between the magnetic grapples.

"—new transmission," a voice crackled over the radio.

"Say again?"

"We just picked up—" Samantha's voice disappeared in bursts of static.

Aton glanced at Malice. She shrugged helplessly.

He turned back to the screens and readouts. "No problems here. You?"

"Looks good."

He found himself sweating in his suit, and upped the cooling unit. Tension was gnawing at him, not so much because of the immediate dangers, more because he felt himself confronting something elemental, a projection from inside himself.

The vehicle lurched and sank suddenly, and the control levers tried to pull out of his hands. "What's happening?" he called to Malice.

"I don't know."

The screen cleared. "We've broken through into a cave." The ship stabilized and the glaring light from the eater diminished as it was temporarily deprived of further rock to fuel its fire. The light was still bright enough, though, to illuminate the deep cavern they were passing through. Boulders cast huge shifting shadows on walls of rock, and in the far distance Aton thought he saw something moving—a creature like an enormous caterpillar, disappearing down a remote tunnel.

That too stirred ersatz memories. But then the eater reached the floor of the cave and chewed into it with a flash and concussion, scattering rock dust and buffeting the ship.

The progress downward continued. Occasionally Aton glanced at the upscreen and saw the tunnel they had carved stretching above them, straight and clean through the rock. The weapons ship was a small black dot silhouetted against the diminishing white circle of daylight.

They passed through more caves, then a section of volcanic rock honeycombed with lava tubes. A sightless creature like an enormous mole was momentarily caught in the eater's glare; Aton glimpsed it charging mindlessly down a passageway, and then it was gone.

For the next fifteen minutes, the ship maintained its descent. It passed through a section of black rock whose higher density slowed the eater; then hit another porous section containing an underground river that exploded in sizzling, hissing steam.

Aton checked a sonogram of the layers of rock beneath. The ship was approaching a point at which the rock seemed to terminate. Beyond that was emptiness—a huge cavity. He turned to Malice. "Should be emerging—" he began.

There was a sudden throbbing inside his head—a crippling pressure, as if his skull was about to burst open. Gasping with the pain, he checked his suit's air indicator. It was normal. He heard Malice cry out and saw her grab her suit helmet in her hands. She tugged at it, pulled it off, and threw it aside. It hit the floor, bounced, and rolled.

She doubled over and fell half out of the couch. Her face was bright red and she was making choking noises. She coughed violently and a plug of thick yellow sputum came out of her mouth.

Aton locked the grapple levers to hold the eater immobile beneath the ship. He stumbled out of his chair, then collapsed to his knees as a new wave of pressure hit him, blurring his vision. He suffered another hallucination—himself and a group of ragged, desperate convicts, the letters MYXO crudely scratched in rock, men collapsing, thick yellow mucus plugging their throats, a voice shouting, demanding that they surrender.

Aton's anger surged up, and the hallucination receded. He clawed his way across the canting deck of the vehicle to Malice. She was in convulsions now, and her face was turning a darker shade of red as she struggled unsuccessfully to breathe.

The shouting voice that he had just hallucinated was in his head again. He felt rage at the invasion, and his anger drove it back. He lurched to the vector controls, corrected the ship's position, and stopped its descent. Then he pulled off his helmet and got down on his knees beside Malice.

Her struggles were growing weaker. Her eyes had rolled up, showing only the whites, and her mouth was completely filled with solidifying mucus. Aton tried to pry it out with his fingers, but the gloves of his suit were too bulky. He bent and pressed his mouth to hers, sucked out a wedge of the thick yellow gunk, and spat it on the floor. The taste was foul, and for a moment he almost vomited. The pain hammered at his temples; he thrust it aside. He sucked from her mouth once more, and spat; then again.

Finally, he pushed hard with his knee in her abdomen and she coughed, ejecting one last great gob of brownish phlegm from her throat. She took urgent breaths. The purple hue of her face began to diminish.

She blinked and focused on him. "I couldn't stop it." Her voice was a dry, painful sound. "It was in my head—"

"I know." The pain was still throbbing at the edges

of his consciousness, but the sense of pressure was diminishing. "I felt it too." He groped for his suit helmet and fixed it back in position, then stumbled to the guidance controls. The eater had strayed out of position, sinking almost out of range of the grapples. The ship was following it, drifting aimlessly—Aton's quick fix of the vector controls had been inaccurate. He felt sweat running down his forehead, stinging his eyes. He blinked it away and let the probe-trained reflexes guide his hands, making fine, delicate adjustments, recapturing control.

But the ship had drifted lower, and the eater had fallen with it. Finally, it broke through.

The screens showed an immense chamber below, perhaps a thousand miles in diameter. At its center, dwarfing the flaring radiance of the mass eater, was a great globular mass of gas, rotating slowly, pulsing with white light.

Aton felt the ship lurch under him as violent air currents escaped from the chamber. The eater was blown to one side, and he almost lost it. Out of the corner of his eye he saw Malice getting back into the pilot's chair, her hands on the controls, calming the violent motion of the ship.

Aton lowered the containment vessel, slowly, delicately toward the mass eater. Its job was done; it had to be recaptured. He nudged it gently toward the vessel's open door.

An alarm sounded inside the ship, and he heard Malice cry out in confusion. Still he concentrated on recapturing the little flaring star below.

"We're losing power," she shouted to him.

He ignored her. The eater hesitated at the mouth of the sphere, then suddenly slipped into place. He slammed the hatch shut and activated the containment field.

As he did so, the main lights went out inside the ship. "What's happening?" he shouted to Malice.

"Some sort of radiation. Maybe electromagnetic pulse. It's killing all the systems, one by one."

He fell sideways as the ship lurched under him. Some of the screens were still working, and showed the ship sinking from the mouth of the shaft, into the chamber. The huge mass of gas pulsed brighter, directly below.

"Get us back up to the rock," he shouted to Malice.

"I'll try."

The ship spun. Aton groped for the manual grapples, originally installed as anchors to secure the ship to floating asteroids. The roof of the chamber swung into view and he fired them toward it, trying to grab it with the metal claws. There was a scraping, grinding noise, then a massive jolt.

"Power down," he shouted to Malice, winching the ship up against the ceiling of rock.

"Right." She flipped switches.

"Get the weapons ship down here."

"It is, already. But it's not responding."

Aton looked at the last active screen. He saw the other vehicle spinning slowly, its attitude thrusters dead. It headed down toward the glowing mass of gas, turning end over end. Its silhouette became a black speck, and was swallowed up.

"I'm going out there," he told her.

She turned and stared at him. "There's nothing you can do."

"We're carrying missiles. The launch systems are dead"—he gestured at the control panel—"but I can detach one and fire it manually." He stepped into the airlock and swung the door shut before she could argue.

Then he was outside, like a fly trying to cling to the ceiling of the enormous chamber. Gravity, here, was a fraction of Earth normal, but still it tried to pull him toward the glowing gas below.

He checked that the grapples were secure, then edged along the upper surface of the ship, gripping handholds in its smooth curved hull. He saw one of the missiles mounted near the rear of the vehicle. Cautiously, he felt his way toward it.

Pain invaded his consciousness again. He fought it, refusing to be deflected from his task.

This was not your role. The words seemed to form themselves in his head. He hallucinated Bedeker's voice and saw his face.

"I'll decide that." Aton reached the missile. He struggled to focus his blurred vision, and reached for the maniple accessory stored in the side pocket of his suit. Clumsily, he fitted it over his right glove.

You and I are the same. We share the pleasure of inflicting pain, of destroying beauty.

Aton fitted the wrench extension of the maniple around the first bolt securing the missile to the ship. A servo motor whined; the bolt spun free. "I don't know who or what you are, Bedeker. But you're wrong."

I am Plasm. I am Chthon.

Aton edged further along. His foot slipped and for a sickening moment he felt his legs swing out and dangle into emptiness. He scrabbled for a handhold and slowly managed to haul himself back to safety, wedging his body in the small gap between the ceiling of rock and the upper surface of the ship. He attached his wrench to the second bolt, and spun it free.

If you kill me, the Minionette dies also.

Pain bloomed again in Aton's skull, and he saw Malice spasming in her chair, her mouth clogged with yellow mucus, her eyes staring up at him imploringly.

He banished the vision, grabbed the missile's mount, and swiveled it on its third and last remaining bolt. He knew it was armed, but there was no way to check the setting of its proximity fuse. A cable ran from underneath the mounting plate, into a grommet in the shell of the ship. Aton switched to a cutting blade. There was a chance he could trigger the system by shorting it. He stabbed the tip of the blade into the cable.

She is dying now.

Rage consumed him, more than ever before. He wrenched the blade in the cable as if he were stabbing the entity that was Bedeker. A spark flashed; the missile fired.

The blast from its rocket motor hit Aton in the chest and smashed him backward, tearing him free from the refuge where he had lodged himself between the rock and the ship. He was momentarily blinded by fire and smoke.

Gravity dragged him down, and he tumbled helplessly. Below him, the missile was a diminishing dot of flame, arcing toward the swirling, glowing gas. It disappeared, and he saw himself following it into oblivion.

Then came a momentary flash as the missile's warhead exploded. It seemed tiny compared to the huge mass of vapor; yet it had an immediate effect. The steady pulsing of the gas became erratic. Electrical discharges spasmed through the mass from one side to another. As Aton fell toward it, he watched it tear itself apart.

Tendrils of gas spiraled free from the core. A shrill, painful screaming invaded Aton's consciousness; then a babble of incoherent sound. The core of the gas blossomed into a fireball, and flashed blinding white.

Aton was seized by the blast like a leaf in a firestorm. Alarms sounded inside his helmet, and status indicators flashed red. He saw the outside of the suit catch fire, and he heard the cooling system overload. He was engulfed in flame; the roiling, burning gas surged up around him, and consumed him.

CHAPTER 18 _____

Nightmare images formed and flickered like heat mirages. Lizard creatures clawing through rock, hissing with rage; men and women dressed in rags, stripping flesh from one another with their teeth and fingernails; a woman brandishing a knife, falling into fire; a man's body bursting open, gushing black blood.

But cool waves were lapping at his body, caressing his skin. Gradually the fever dreams were washed away, until, finally, he opened his eyes.

"Don't try to move."

He recognized the voice. He saw her face looking down at him, young yet intently serious. "Samantha," he murmured.

She smiled faintly as if she liked hearing him speak her name. "You're in a burn tank," she told him. "By the time we got to you, your suit's cooling system was shot. You were just about fried."

"Bedeker—"

"You took care of it. Don't worry. You'll be out in a few hours, with a new skin. It's half grown already."

Her words fell into his mind with a steady rhythm, like rain. He started to drift again—then remembered. "Malice," he said. His eyes opened wide.

Samantha's smile wavered. "We saved her too." She straightened up, and her face moved out of focus. "You'd better sleep, now."

Aton felt something touch his arm, and he lost consciousness. This time, there were no dreams.

"One is pleased by your wholeness," said Srndhi.

Aton flexed his muscles. The clothes felt almost painfully rough against his soft, new skin. He looked down at his hands. The flesh was unlined, baby-pink. The entire accelerated healing process, using catalyzed cells, had taken less than a day.

"One was referring not to your body, but to your mental condition," the alien corrected him. "A catharsis has occurred."

"Really?" He was finding it hard to concentrate, feeling restless, impatient to see Malice.

The door opened. Aton looked up quickly, and she was there.

This time, she showed no hesitation or reserve. She stepped toward him, her eyes watching him intently. As she came closer, she smiled; and then, when she was just a couple of feet away, she burst into laughter.

Aton was momentarily confused. "What's the joke?"

She clapped her hands. "There's no joke. I'm just happy." She sat opposite him, still staring intently at his face. "I was sure you had been killed. Then when Samantha said they'd found you drifting in the chamber in the center of the planet, and you were still alive, I thought you'd be maimed for life. But you're not, you're—reborn." She kissed him suddenly on the mouth.

"But I thought *you* were dead," Aton told her. "The Bedeker consciousness—if that's what it was—said it was killing you."

"A deception," said Srndhi. "One was monitoring events on the telepathic band. Unfortunately, because of interference, one was unable to send reassuring information by radio. While you were readying the missile, Aton, the consciousness was directing all its energies on yourself. You were the only threat; thus it ignored Malice."

"I guess I should have figured that. It really was Bedeker, was it?"

"Yes. But please come to the control room, for further information."

Together, Aton and the Minionette followed Srndhi out of the cabin.

The control room of the Earth ship was as Aton remembered it: black consoles, brushed aluminum, white ceramics. The face of Chthon still loomed outside the viewports.

"Well, well. Back from the dead," Samantha greeted him. She examined his new skin with professional interest. There was no trace, now, of the mixed emotions he had seen in her face when he had first regained consciousness.

"Somehow I didn't expect—still to be so close to Chthon." Aton gestured at the disk of the planet.

"I'm still gathering data," she told him. "It's a habit I just can't seem to shake." She went over to the starcube. "Want to see a replay?"

They gathered around the display. It showed Chthon much as it looked outside the viewports now, a blue-green sphere streaked with white, turning slowly against a background of stars.

"You braked out of your polar orbit and the weapons ship followed you down," she said. Simultaneously, two points of light appeared in the cube, arcing toward the planet's surface.

"You tunneled in, and we lost contact. Then Srndhi's equipment picked up a powerful TP transmission. The Chthon/Bedeker consciousness—call it plasm; that's what it called itself—had detected your presence. It was appealing for help from the extragalactic entities, whose exact nature we still don't understand."

"I remember, you tried to warn us," said Aton. "We picked up fragments of your radio message."

"Yeah. Well, by this time I was feeling kind of sick, sitting on my hands out in space, while you guys were doing all the work." She sounded embarrassed. "So, I came down after you."

"A deed of courage and friendship," Srndhi said.

She turned on him. "Will you cut it out?" She paused, recovering her cool. "Anyhow, we moved in."

The picture in the cube shifted and grew larger, focusing on the hole in the planet's crust.

"By this time, the surveillance systems in the weapons ship that followed you down had all gone dead," Samantha continued. "And our monitors were picking up nothing from your ship either. The plasm entity had hit you with a chain of pulses powerful enough to override your shield and knock out most of your electric systems. Although it waited till you'd put the eater back in its containment vessel; it knew that thing would be a liability if it ran wild inside Chthon.

"So I was in low orbit, figuring I'd follow you down the hole you'd dug, when this happened." The display showed a jet of white-hot gas streaming out of the cavity. "Your missile destabilized the plasm, and it blew up." The picture pulled back, showing the gas streaming into space, dispersing into a formless cloud, drifting away toward the stars.

"After that," Samantha finished, "we went in and pulled you both out."

"But what was this—plasm?" Malice asked.

"The planet Chthon has an extremely powerful magnetic field," Srndhi said. "It also has much volcanic activity. An evolution occurred, of a mineral intelligence. Possibly at first it was in liquid form; if so, it gradually evolved and changed its state. We found it as a plasma: ionized gas at high temperature, contained in the hollow core of the planet. By 'plasm,' it referred to itself as a plasma life form.

"It maintained control over all biological life in Chthon. Decades ago, one of the convicts—a man named Charles Bedeker—strayed deeper than anyone else had ever ventured. Plasm took over his mind and body, seeing in him an opportunity to spread its malign influence to other worlds.

"It directed him to large natural deposits of mineral wealth, then enabled his escape. The genetic laboratories on Luna were financially vulnerable, and free from any governmental controls. Bedeker worked there for thirty years, as an extension of the plasm consciousness, which controlled him like a dumb terminal.

"Subsequently, it made contact with extragalactic mineral entities, which offered the potential power to exterminate biological life entirely." The Xest paused. "One's own race is now in communication with these extragalactic entities. The plasm had been their sole source of information—there is no biological life in their galaxy—and they had not realized it is possible for carbon-based life to acquire intelligence. They regret having tampered. In due course, we hope for a mutually beneficial understanding."

"Samantha," a voice interrupted.

She looked up. "What is it, Tomas?"

The tall, blond, handsome Sim nodded politely to Aton and to Malice. "Excuse me for interrupting. Samantha, the analysis is complete. The data is in. Central wants to head back to Luna. With all our firepower here, the home base is unprotected. That conflicts with fundamental priorities."

She stood up. "I guess it would. Well, you both know the score now, right?"

"Yes." Aton nodded thoughtfully. "I suppose there's no way this—plasm—could reconstitute itself?"

"It existed in precarious equilibrium within its magnetic field," said Srndhi, "which is why the small warhead that you fired was sufficient to disrupt it. Now that it has dispersed into the vacuum of space, one cannot see how it might become anything other than an inert cloud of gas."

"So are you people coming back to Luna with us, or what?" Samantha asked. She was waiting with her hands on her hips, in the same impatient pose as when Aton had first seen her, outside the jail cell on the moon.

"One has much to report to one's people," the Xest said. "One's own ship is still nearby, under control of the smaller self. With regret, it is time to depart."

"Well, I figured as much," said Samantha. "Too bad; I enjoyed arguing with you, Srndhi." She turned to Aton and the Minionette. "What about you two?"

Malice looked at Aton. "I know you have no wish to return to Minion," she said softly.

"I was thinking," he said, "that we should go to Hvee. My father was never able to confide in me, about our—family history. When I left, he was in poor health." He looked steadily at Malice, carefully controlling his emotions. "I would like, before he dies, to tell him that I know now what happened, between him and you."

She inclined her head. "As you wish,"

Samantha was watching them with frank curiosity. "Interesting," she said. "But I guess it's none of my business, right?" She turned without waiting for them to answer. "Srndhi, can they hitch a ride with you?"

The Xest walked to the starcube and tapped out a series of coordinates with one of its legs. The face of Chthon disappeared, and an image of the galaxy took its place. Colored arcs sprang into existence between the stars. "It would be a simple matter to take you to Hvee," Srndhi concluded, "on the way to the Xest home world, provided the smallness of one's space vehicle will not cause too much discomfort."

"Good enough," said Samantha.

"But what about you?" Malice asked her. "You seemed troubled before we reached Chthon. Does it bother you to return to Luna?"

Samantha gave her a guarded look. "I'm fine," she said shortly. She folded her arms across her slim body, as if placing a barrier between herself and the Minionette. "I got a lot of work to do back there, anyway. Maybe some changes to suggest to Central." She paused, choosing her words carefully. "The way Srndhi says it, if people don't have the intellectual or physical capacity to take advantage of their freedoms, they're not really free. I hate to have to admit it, but that is a valid point."

"We're almost ready, Samantha," Tomas called to her from one of the consoles. "The last of the convicts have been found."

"Convicts?" Aton asked. He walked over to the screen in front of Tomas and looked down at the picture it was displaying.

"Slightly more than fifty convicts escaped," Tomas explained. "The hole that you excavated with the mass eater connected with some of the tunnels in their underground prison. They managed to climb to the surface."

The screen showed men and women being herded by robots toward a small tracked vehicle. The convicts were shouting futile abuse and throwing rocks at the machines. One of them tried to make a break; the police robot snared him with a net, and hauled him back.

"You should release them," said Aton. Without knowing why, he saw himself down there on the surface of the planet, sharing their anger and helplessness.

"They're sociopaths," Samantha reminded him.

"Murderers, most of them. In many other systems, they'd be put to death."

"But they're still people," Aton said. "Why not leave them outside on the surface of the planet? Let that be their prison. Turn Idyllia over to them."

Samantha laughed. "Neat idea, but—"

"Idyllia is privately owned," Tomas pointed out.

"Pay for it by selling off the remainder of Bedeker's equipment in the gene labs," Aton replied.

Samantha gave Aton a wry, condescending look. "The universe doesn't work this way. You don't get something for nothing. If you commit crimes, if you kill people, you have to pay."

"There's been enough punishment," he told her. "And you seem to be forgetting an old-fashioned idea. Redemption."

"Aton is right," said Srndhi. "Ethically speaking—"

"Okay, okay!" Samantha held up her hands. "We'll let Central deal with it. Tomas, check it out."

The Sim stood silently for a moment, communicating with the centralized artificial intelligence via his radio data link. Then he shrugged. "There would be no conflict with the basic precepts, provided the convicts remain exiled from other Federation worlds."

"Hm." Samantha drummed her fingers on the control panel. "But I still don't like it."

"I liberated the planet from the plasm," Aton reminded her. "Perhaps you could see this as payment to me."

She looked at him with her eyes narrowed, and something indefinable passed between him and her. "All right," she said slowly. "Yes; that's exactly how I'll think of it. Tomas, go ahead."

"One moment." He paused. "There." He gestured to the screen.

The robot cops were turning away from their prisoners, showing no further interest in them. The ragged men and women were standing and staring, unable to believe what was happening to them. One of them backed off a few paces, then turned and started to run. Hesitantly at first, the others began to follow.

The ragged human figures dispersed across the hillside, heading for a forest in the distance. Faintly, over the audio link, came the sound of shouts and cheering.

"Satisfied?" Samantha asked Aton.

He took her hand. Before, it had felt strong; this time, it seemed fragile. "Thank you," he told her.

Her face showed mixed emotions, as if she was disconcerted by his touch. Abruptly, she pulled free. "Tomas will show you the way out," she said. She stepped back a couple of paces. "I've never been big on saying good-bye."

The last Aton saw of her, she was mating the end of a cable to her neck implant, preparing to download more data.

CHAPTER 19 ⎯⎯⎯⎯

The Xest ship set down on an open, grassy hillside. It was dawn on Hvee; the air was cool and the sky was gray-blue with early light.

Srndhi and the smaller Xest followed Aton and Malice to the ship's exit. "One regrets this parting," the alien said. "Although, of course, the cells remember."

"Maybe you should stay here on Hvee for a couple of days," Aton suggested.

Srndhi peered out of the hatch. "A most agreeable world," it commented. "But one has a duty to one's race. Still, one senses our timelines will cross again."

Aton and Malice descended the ramp to the ground. The grass was beaded with dew, and Aton smelled Hvee flowers growing in a nearby field.

He turned with Malice and waved to Srndhi. The small Xest had climbed on top of the larger one, as if to get a better view. Solemnly, each of the aliens raised a leg in farewell.

Then the ramp retracted and the hatch closed. As Aton and Malice stood and watched, the ship lifted silently into the morning sky and drifted up, disappearing from view.

Aton looked around at the landscape. "It's four years or more, since I was here," he said.

"You recognize where you are?" She had a teasing, playful expression, as if she was holding a secret.

"I'm not sure. We seem to be some distance from my house. Why did you tell Srndhi to set us down here?"

She took his hand. "Come. I'll show you."

He followed her across the soft grass toward some woodland nearby. As the dawn light brightened, the air became filled with birdsong.

"This isn't the way to my home," he complained.

"I know."

"But I want us to see Aurelius. That was the point in coming here."

"Your father won't even be awake yet," she pointed out. "We have at least an hour to ourselves. Are you sure you don't recognize where you are?"

He was following her between tall trees, across a springy carpet of ferns and moss. The smell of vegetation was rich and strong. "Yes; I used to walk through these woods when I was a child."

She paused, looking around as if to check her bearings, then led him along a tiny path that was almost completely overgrown with bushes.

They emerged in a glade; and now he remembered. Tall grass and wild Hvee flowers grew here, and there was the faint sound of a small stream running close by. The trees cut off all sight of the outside world, making this a special, secret place.

She went quickly to a tree stump near the center of the clearing, sat down, and searched in the grass at her feet. "Here," she said, plucking a Hvee flower and holding it out to him.

Aton stepped forward, struck dumb by the flood of memories. He felt as if he were walking to her in slow time. The glade had seemed much larger when he had been seven years old, and he had been lost and unsure of himself, then. But the Minionette had not changed; she was as radiant and compelling as ever.

He took the flower from her hand.

"It lives," she told him. "Proving my love."

"Put it in my hair," he told her, "as you did before."

She stood up, moving lightly on her feet. Her eyes were alive with anticipation. "You are so much taller now," she said, smiling, reaching up to tuck the blossom above his ear. "There."

He looked down at her. Conflicting emotions surged in him and he felt dizzy. Still with a sense of moving in slow motion, he reached for her. "You told me I would never again meet anyone as beautiful as you. You told me no one would ever kiss me again as you did then."

She parted her lips, breathing deeply. "Was it true?"

"Of course it was true!" His tension broke and he shook her by her shoulders. "You gave me no choice!

You knew exactly how to manipulate my emotions." He drew a deep breath. "Even now, you still do. You knew how it would affect me, to bring me back to this place." His grip tightened. "Isn't that so?"

"Yes." She was watching him intently, savoring his inner conflict. "It's true. I did it deliberately. Are you angry with me?"

"Temptress." He shook her violently. "You corrupted me."

She gave a little gasp.

He slapped her face, and the skin turned pink, showing the outline of his hand. She fell against him and pressed her body close, trembling with excitement.

He seized her by her hair and tilted her head back, then kissed her angrily. At last, the ghost of his past was exorcised; he was no longer haunted by the image of himself as a young boy, helpless and afraid.

"*Now* pledge yourself to me," he told her.

She sank down on her knees in front of him. "I am yours," she said simply. "Your anger is my passion; your hate is my love."

He stared at her, remembering when such a statement would have made him despise himself for the perverse, obscene fantasies it roused. He remembered, too, how he had punished others for his own sense of shame.

Now, however, he felt no guilt—only a fierce satisfaction at having confronted and vanquished the specters that had haunted him for so long. He would always carry the stigma of his genes, as a disorder that could never be erased; yet he was redeemed.

The caves of Chthon seemed far away, remote in

space and time, as he pushed the Minionette down onto the soft grass of the forest glade. This was a singular moment, isolated not only from the past but from the future. Despite her pledge, he sensed there could be no guarantees, and the dark side of his soul might yet return to tempt him toward self-destruction. For now, however, the moment was enough.

ABOUT THE AUTHOR

Charles Platt's science fiction includes *Twilight of the City*, a study of urban decay at the turn of the century, and *Less Than Human* (under the pseudonym Robert Clarke), which applies a humorous treatment to traditional SF themes. His nonfiction includes computer books and the highly praised *Dream Makers* series, profiling fifty-seven of the best known science fiction authors in the field.

Platt is the onetime editor of *New Worlds*, a radical British magazine of the late 1960s. He now lives in New York City, where in addition to writing novels, he is science fiction editor for the publisher Franklin Watts.